"WHAT'S THE MATTER, JONATHAN?"

"Why would anything be the matter?" he returned coolly.

"You just seem . . . annoyed with me." Her eyes held his, searching for a clue but finding none.

He looked away from her. "I have some business matters on my mind. Some calls to make while I'm here," he mumbled, his eyes clouded with thought.

Dissatisfied, Cynthia pursued the matter further. "Without sounding too naive, I thought that that was one of Suzanne's jobs."

"I take care of my own business. Never forget that," he boomed, then added in a lower though equally venomous tone, "and my own affairs have nothing to do with you!"

CANDLELIGHT ECSTASY CLASSIC ROMANCES

CANDLELIGHT ECSTASY ROMANCES®

SURRENDER BY MOONLIGHT

Bonnie Drake

A CANDLELIGHT ECSTASY CLASSIC ROMANCE

Published by
Dell Publishing Co., Inc.
1 Dag Hammarskjold Plaza
New York, New York 10017

Dell ® TM 681510, Dell Publishing Co., Inc.

A Candlelight Ecstasy Classic Romance

Candlelight Ecstasy Romance®, 1,203,540, is a registered trademark of Dell Publishing Co., Inc.

ISBN: 0-440-18426-6

Printed in the United States of America

One Previous Edition

December 1986

10 9 8 7 6 5 4 3 2 1

WFH

To Our Readers:

By popular demand we are happy to announce that we will be bringing you two Candlelight Ecstasy Classic Romances every month.

In the upcoming months your favorite authors and their earlier best-selling Candlelight Ecstasy Romances® will be available once again.

As always, we will continue to present the distinctive sensuous love stories that you have come to expect only from Ecstasy and also the very finest work from new authors of contemporary romantic fiction.

Your suggestions and comments are always welcome. Please write to us at the address below.

Sincerely,

The Editors
Candlelight Romances
1 Dag Hammarskjold Plaza
New York, New York 10017

CHAPTER ONE

The telephone continued to ring as Cynthia looked up from her papers. Five . . . six . . . seven . . . *when will whoever that is decide that I'm not home*, she asked herself angrily. Eight . . . nine . . . *oh, hell*, she swore under her breath as she slammed down her pencil and crossed the room to yield to the persistent caller. The phone had been ringing on and off all day, preventing her from reaching the deadline she had set for herself. But letting it ring endlessly was almost as distracting as answering it, she was quick to discover.

"Hello!" she barked in frustration into the receiver, the brunt of her annoyance to be borne by this one unfortunate soul. There was a brief pause at the other end before the deep, unsure voice began.

"Ah . . . is Professor Blake there?"

Instant recognition lit up Cynthia's face. "Uncle William? It's I!" she exclaimed, her tone reflecting the smile which suddenly warmed her features.

"Cindy? It didn't sound like you at all! Are you all right?" William Thorpe's concern was obvious and Cynthia chided herself for having answered the phone as she had.

7

"I'm fine, Uncle William, just busy. I can't seem to get any of this work done. If it isn't one thing, it's the next, between the phone and the doorbell and . . . well, you know how it is. You're busy enough yourself." She sprawled out on the sofa for a much needed stretch after maintaining the tense position at her desk for so long.

"Busy is putting it mildly, Cindy! But I haven't spoken to you in so long, I thought I'd give you a call. How've you been?" His voice had regained the confident boom that Cynthia knew and loved so well. She warmed as she heard it, sensing the security that Uncle William always held for her.

"Everything's great here, just hectic. I'm trying to make up my final exam to get it to the secretary for typing by Wednesday; at the same time, I've got fifty papers to grade and more figures to compile for my dissertation. If I make it to commencement exercises, it'll be a miracle!" she laughed, knowing full well that she had always managed to get everything done on time in the past and would do so again this semester.

"When *is* commencement this year?" he asked, with a pointedness which made Cynthia wonder.

"May twenty-fourth!" she exclaimed, entranced with the sound of it. The date held a magical charm for her, as had each commencement since she'd been teaching these three years, as when she'd been a student herself. While the rest of the world divided the calendar year either by the seasons, the major holidays, the paycheck, or the fiscal year, the world of academia saw it from vacation to vacation— from Labor Day to Thanksgiving to Christmas to intersession to April vacation to commencement—with a paper or exam to be ground out before each break.

The booming voice returned, "May twenty-fourth? That's only a few weeks off! I guess you've got your work cut out for you between now and then!" He laughed, knowing that Cynthia loved her work, despite its steady

8

demands. "What are your plans after that, Cindy? Any ideas for the summer?" Again, she had the feeling that he was leading up to something.

Cynthia did not see or talk with her uncle all that often, but when she did it was always a warm, gratifying, and reassuring contact, usually with a definite objective in the mind of at least one of them. And she loved him for it, as one can only love someone who is there when you need him, in the background when you don't.

Hugging her knees to her chest as a substitute for her uncle, she giggled affectionately. "What are you getting at, Uncle William? I smell a scheme brewing in that devious lawyer's brain of yours. What's up your sleeve?"

He joined her with an amused chuckle. "Thank goodness the prosecution cannot see through me as easily as you do." They both laughed, before he continued. "Actually, this particular scheme was hatched by the other side itself!"

"OK, let's have it!" she urged, her curiosity aroused to hear Uncle William's latest. Over the years, she had learned to appreciate his schemes, which had taken her, among other places, to London as a companion to one of his elderly clients, to the West Coast as the chaperone to the teenaged daughter of another, to South America as his own personal secretary on a particular case, and so on. Now that she thought of it, he had managed to provide a trip for her almost every year since her mother's death had made him her closest living relative.

As though in the courtroom, Uncle William cleared his throat and launched his opening argument. "My dear Cynthia, the school year is just about over and you could use a rest. A perfect solution was just offered to me . . . er, you. How does three months on an isolated island off the coast of Maine strike you? No telephone. No doorbell. No distractions. Lots of peace and quiet . . ."

"I'll take it! Where do I sign?" blurted Cynthia, immediately adoring the thought of solitude and escape from the city sounds that serenaded her apartment day and night.

Typically, Uncle William was not yet finished with his address. His powerful voice continued over the line as though she had never interrupted it. "There's a small island five miles offshore which has two cottages on it. The owner of the island lives in one, the other is vacant. Just waiting for you, Cindy!"

She was quickly becoming suspicious, as she realized that the offer was legitimate. "Waiting for me to do what, Uncle William?"

"House-sit, my dear! It seems this gentleman who owns the place will be on and off it himself all summer, but wants someone to keep an eye on things while he's not there."

A possibility suddenly dawned on Cynthia. "You mean, he wants a house-sitter or a housekeeper?" she asked skeptically. "I have enough trouble remembering to make my own bed each day, with all the other work I've got, let alone having to make someone else's!"

"No, no, house-sitting is all . . . no cleaning . . . no cooking . . . no housekeeping at all. Just being there and, as I was told, keeping your eyes open." he elaborated patiently, well used to Cynthia's indignant outburst against custodial work.

"Sounds very suspicious," she murmured, her forefinger tapping her lower lip, as she tried to put the puzzle pieces together. "Where did you hear about this, Uncle William?"

His voice lowered in mock mystery. "The other side," he drawled slowly, then proceeded at a normal pace to show her that it was an honest offer. "Through the years, I have become friendly with John Cummings over at the DEA. As a matter of fact, didn't you meet him once with me—yes, when I was defending that Stanton boy against drug smuggling charges? Do you remember?"

Cynthia pulled herself upright on the sofa, becoming

10

more serious as the conversation had. She drew her brown eyebrows together as she searched her memory, then her eyes lit up in recognition. "Sure! He was the agent on the case. Kind of an easygoing fellow, as I recall. I liked him, even though he was your opponent," she smiled. "But what does the Drug Enforcement Administration have to do with my summer?" she added, perplexed.

"Nothing at all, Cindy. I just happened to be talking to John and he mentioned this fellow—the owner of the island—who was looking for someone responsible and did I know of any law student or somebody like that who would be free for the summer." He sounded slightly leading, and Cynthia couldn't stifle the chuckle that his suggestiveness inspired.

"And what did my good uncle tell him?"

William was not one to be daunted by her smugness, as he went on boldly. "I told him that I had just the right person for the job. A Professor Blake, from the Community College, who was working on a doctoral dissertation and would appreciate the opportunity for the uninterrupted peace which the island could promise. I even said that I would personally vouch for the Professor's background and reliability."

"Thank you, sir," she replied affectionately. "Obviously you informed him neither that Professor Blake was your niece nor that Professor Blake was a woman?" she asked, relatively confident of the answer.

Cynthia knew that her uncle's usually ruddy complexion would be even more pink by now; he always blushed when being found out. Confirming her suspicion, he cleared his throat again and murmured softly, "No need. No need, my dear. Everything I told him was the truth. He never asked about the other details." Always the stickler for technicalities, her Uncle William was! "At any rate," he continued, "he thinks highly enough of me to take my recommendation. The job is yours if you want it . . . but they want someone installed on the island by the first of June. Any problem?"

Cynthia laughed at his command of the situation, though it was another of his traits she loved. As independent as she was, she did enjoy—once in a while—to have a decision made for her, especially by someone she trusted as much as she did her uncle.

"I guess not!" She shrugged her shoulders, amazed that the solution to her problem had been so simple. "I was just going to stay around here working all summer. But with the noise and the interruptions, it could have been a real problem!"

She paused, an odd unsureness gnawing at her. "Uncle William," she began tentatively, "this whole thing sounds very mysterious. Are you sure it's on the level? I mean, it sounds too good to be true. But why did John Cummings approach you? Who is this nameless landowner? What am I supposed to be on the lookout for? It all sounds very fishy . . . literally and figuratively," she laughed, as though to dispel her own qualms with a bit of humor.

"You know everything I do, Cindy. The details will all be forthcoming. But I do trust John. Anyway, he knows what a big mouth I have and I'm sure he'd hesitate to pull the wool over my eyes for that reason. I have a certain amount of pull higher up, you know." The attorney's tone was so confident that Cynthia couldn't help but absorb some of his assurance.

"Ah! Of course you're right! I don't know why I'm being so dramatic. Must be too much television!" she laughed heartily, knowing, as did Uncle William, that she didn't own a set. "Tell John that he's got his man . . . er, sitter," she joked again.

The practical side of the lawyer emerged now. "Do you have the papers and books you'll need? Can you do without a library?"

His questions brought a momentary frown to Cynthia's

12

gentle features and she subconsciously twirled her stick-straight brown hair around her finger as she pondered the answer. "I don't know . . . I have all the research done and the raw data are gathered. I can run the comparisons on the computer before I go . . ." Then she brightened as the solution appeared before her. "I know! I've got most of what I need. But I'm sure that this mysterious island-owner won't mind if I take a day off here and there to go to a library. Even Maine must have a good library somewhere!"

Now William was in his element again, the traveler, knowledgeable about all trivia such as local schools and libraries. "Orono! Not far inland from where you'll be. That's where the university is. Perfect! Why don't you contact them before you go?"

One last time, Cynthia grew pensive. She spoke more slowly, reluctant to let the excitement carry her away. "Yes . . . I suppose I could . . . but, Uncle William . . . where is the hitch? I keep feeling there must be one. How much rent does the old miser want?" Her eyes narrowed at the last.

A low chuckle echoed across the telephone line. "Tut, tut, Cindy. I thought you were a liberal thinker. No unfair judgments, remember? No one said anything about an 'old miser.' And the rent is minimal, much less than you're paying now. You're doing a job, simple as it may be. Low rent. No pay. A fairly even deal. You supply your own food, but that's about it." He hesitated for an instant, wondering if she would find some other kink to iron out. At her silence, he pushed on. "What do you say, Cynthia? It would really be good for you! The timing is perfect . . . everything." He paused again.

Cynthia struggled to find some logical reason to refuse the offer, but other than the illogical gut suspicion she had, she could find none, particularly when her uncle's voice came low and mischievous over the wire. "Do you think

13

you can manage without Professor Wittson for the summer?"

"Uncle William, you're impossible!" she shot back at him, then grinned. "If I didn't know better, I'd think you have your detectives following me around. They may see me dating Geoffrey, but they don't know what happens during those dates . . . ," she teased.

Stricken by shyness at this turn in the conversation, William cleared his throat again before venturing softly, "Are you serious about him, Cindy?"

Her answer was quick, forceful, and completely honest. "No! He's a good friend of mine. Oh, I think he'd like it a little differently, but that's the way it is. And his phone calls are interrupting my work as much as everyone else's . . . present company excluded, of course!" she added generously.

"Cindy, you really should slow down. You should date more, you know. The right man would be good for you." His concern touched her, although they'd been through the discussion many times before and he knew not to pursue it further.

"I know, Uncle William. I really don't have time right now for that. Soon enough!" She pacified him subtly, without lying too blatantly. The truth was that she hadn't found a male companion who interested her more than her work, and until that day came, she was content to spend her nights alone. Geoffrey fascinated her in some ways. A Professor of English, he was constantly challenging her intellectually, taking her to the theater, suggesting books for her to read, and then discussing them with her. He was eager to study when she did, providing her with companionship, silent and patient, at the library or at one of their apartments. But she felt no physical attraction to him, and as timid as his overtures were in that respect, she was unable to respond.

Ever the expert at bringing the conversation full circle,

14

William did so again. "Well, my dear, you will have more time if I let you get off this phone. So it's settled, is it? Can I tell John that his 'old miser' has a house-sitter?" He chuckled good-naturedly and she found herself laughing along with him.

"Yes, Uncle William. The 'old miser' has his house-sitter. And you are a dear for thinking of me! What would I ever do without you?" She meant every word and hoped that her uncle knew that.

"Without me, my dear, you would be forced to find yourself some other debonair bachelor to take over! But," he continued gently, "you know I'll always be here, Cindy."

A sudden tightness formed at the back of Cynthia's throat as the strength of the affection she felt for her uncle surged upward. "I love you, Uncle William," she managed to croak, before she regained her control. Suddenly a thought hit her like a bolt out of the blue. "But where do I go from here? Details . . . where is this island? How do I get there? Shouldn't I speak to someone?"

William's calmness soothed her sudden excitement. "No, no. I'll take care of everything from my end. I'm leaving tomorrow to handle a case in Miami. Probably be gone for three or four days. We'll get together for dinner one evening before you go. I can give you all the instructions then. That is," his voice lowered a notch or two, "if you can spare some time for *this* debonair bachelor . . ."

"Any time, Uncle William. You know that!" she chided, then added with a giggle, "As long as it's after May twenty-fourth!"

Cynthia remained deep in thought about her uncle long after she had hung up the phone. *What a wonderful man,* she thought. *He always comes through for me, doesn't he?* Yes, William Thorpe had indeed come through for her many times during the past nine years. Her own father had died when she was ten, and even then Uncle William had filled the void, perhaps for himself as well as for her. But when her mother had died seven years later, just when she was at the crossroads between high school and college, he had become a major force in her life, encouraging her to enter the university, then becoming involved in that very education.

Although she had her own apartment off campus, they spent much time together discussing her interests as well as his. As a very successful and well-respected trial lawyer, whose reputation far exceeded the limits of Philadelphia, where he kept his main office, his specialty was in handling drug-related cases, a field which interested Cynthia also. It came as no surprise to either of them when she graduated magna cum laude in Sociology and then entered the doctorate program in the same field, specializing in Criminology. Her outstanding performance in graduate school earned her the position she now held as an Assistant Professor of Sociology, one which would undoubtedly be improved once her dissertation was completed and her PhD awarded.

The bubble of her daydream popped abruptly at the thought of her dissertation, and her eyes shot instinctively toward the shelves full of papers, which contained her life's work, or so she saw it. Two years of interviews and tests of drug abusers, painstakingly obtained across prison tables, much made possible by William Thorpe and the leads he gave her. But now, the baby was all hers. As much as Uncle William knew about drug users and abusers, he knew nothing about collecting and analyzing data. That was her own strength. Well, here she was, with reams of information collected and waiting for analysis.

The more she thought about it, the more ideal this island proposal appeared. What she did need more than anything else was time, uninterrupted! That she would have aplenty in the situation Uncle William had described.

If only she could shake the strange feeling of unease at

the aura of perfection surrounding the situation. Her uncle had seemed so sure that it would work out well . . . why did she have such nagging doubts? There were so many unanswered questions. Well, she rationalized, Uncle William would have all the answers before she left. All she had to do was to sit back and let him make the arrangements.

How ludicrous, she laughed aloud as she dragged herself off the padded comfort of the sofa and headed for the desk once more, to picture herself sitting back! That would be wishful thinking, she mused, as she returned to the half-composed final exam which glared at her from the typewriter. If only students knew that it was as painful to make them as to take them! Sighing aloud, she resumed her steady pounding of the keys.

During the few days following her uncle's call, Cynthia found herself, in those rare leisure moments, looking more and more favorably on his suggestion, indeed becoming increasingly excited at the prospect of spending her summer on the island. Several times she thought to call Geoffrey to share the plans with him, but each time she rejected the idea in the belief that such an impulse would give more credence to the seriousness of the relationship than she wanted. Rather, it was three days later, on Friday evening, when they went out for dinner together, that she broke the news.

"I've got great news, Geoffrey," she began, once they had been seated at an intimate corner table at Mario's and the waiter had taken their order for wine.

"So have I!" His own eyes, behind his horn-rimmed glasses, were lit up with an excitement comparable to hers, something unusual for Geoffrey, she thought. "Ladies before gentlemen . . ." he smiled, making a graceful bowing gesture with his slender arm.

Simple gestures such as this always pleased Cynthia.

Not that she had to be the first to share her news, but she admired Geoffrey's ability to be chivalrous without being chauvinistic. He clearly treated her as an equal intellectually, yet he gave deference to her as a woman in a nonpatronizing way.

"I've actually made plans for the summer," she started enthusiastically, hoping that her high spirit would help ease the disappointment she expected from him. "I'm going back to nature, on a remote little island off the coast of Maine. It will be just me—no temptations, no distractions. I think I'll actually be able to get my dissertation done! Doesn't that sound promising?" Her brown eyes opened wide, desperately urging him to share her conviction.

As she had anticipated, however, Geoffrey's face fell, pricking her conscience as it did so. He was a good-looking man, tall and thin, dark-haired, always neat, clean, and pleasantly dressed. Nothing flashy, but very respectable. In fact, Cynthia's only complaint about his looks was that he was too serious. There were no laugh lines on his face to show that he occasionally did enjoy himself. When they first sat down and he had mentioned a surprise of his own, his face had radiated a warmth that flattered him. Cynthia was sorry to see its disappearance now.

"Is this definite?" She nodded. "When did it come up?" he questioned her, taken aback by the suddenness of her plans.

Cynthia told him the whole story, "old miser" and all, in an attempt to convince him, as she convinced herself, of the hope for the summer.

He still seemed startled. "But you know nothing about this place. Or about its owner, for that matter. You don't even know where it is!"

She had grilled herself with the same questions during the past few days, but each time had resolved the quandary as she did now before Geoffrey. "Uncle William is making

18

all of the arrangements. That's his forte. He's been responsible for most of my traveling in the past and I trust him explicitly!" She smiled reassuringly.

A sense of resignation flooded Geoffrey's features, and a sad smile flitted over his lips. "So you'd desert me for the whole summer?"

Once again Cynthia felt a pang of affection for Geoffrey, and she reached her hand over to clasp his fist. "Oh, Geoffrey. It's not like that and you know it! I want to get this work done once and for all. Given the choice between my sweltering apartment in the city and this isolated cottage . . . well, there really is no choice. You understand, don't you?"

Even as her eyes begged for his acceptance, Cynthia realized that it was this aspect of their relationship which, in large part, stifled any physical entanglement. Just as he made her feel like a woman in some respects, in too many others he made her feel positively maternal. Geoffrey was a good ten years older than she was, yet he still needed to be coaxed along in some things like a child. Perhaps it was, among other things, her own strength of character that attracted her to him. Cynthia doubted whether Geoffrey would be strong enough to care for her when the inevitable chinks in her coat of armor were put to the test. No, as fond as she was of Geoffrey and as much as she respected him intellectually, she knew one day she would need more.

The waiter brought a bottle of white wine to the table, filled each glass, and departed. To her chagrin, Geoffrey raised his glass and spoke solemnly. "I'd like to propose a toast . . . to your summer and your island. May they fulfill your expectations . . . and bring you back, freer, to me." Cynthia quickly lifted her glass and sipped the sweet liquid to hide her sudden annoyance. She had almost hoped he would put up an argument about her leaving, fight for her time, something. But his taut acceptance, as

19

much as it irked her time and time again, was something to which she had grown accustomed in the six months they had been dating.

Eager to brighten the atmosphere, Cynthia reproached him. "Come on, Geoffrey. What about your news? You're not going to keep me waiting forever, are you?"

He looked down at his hand gently turning the stem of the wine glass before him. When he glanced up, his eyes were serious and he spoke in a low, even voice. "My news has just been rendered non-news." He smiled sadly before continuing. "I got hold of a place up in Vermont for the month of July and wondered if you'd join me there. But it seems you'll be otherwise occupied." There was a heavy silence, Cynthia dismayed by the bitterness which tinged his words, something with which she wasn't sure how to cope.

"You make me feel like an absolute ogre," she replied, again the tug at her heart telling her how badly she felt to see Geoffrey disappointed. "Oh, I'd love to, Geoffrey, but now that these plans are set . . . I really have to get that work done!"

Geoffrey nervously pushed the glasses further up on his nose as he looked directly at her, a slight anger in his eyes. "I was hoping you'd take a break from your work for just a little bit." The suggestion was there, making Cynthia all the more grateful that she had a solid excuse for not joining him. The last thing she wanted was an intimate few weeks alone, day and night, with Geoffrey. She was only too well aware of the limitations on her feelings toward him, and it would hurt her all the more to make him aware of them. There would be no way to possibly avoid that on such a vacation, particularly given his pointed glance at her now.

She smiled at him, her warmest, most affectionate smile. "I really do appreciate the thought. But I couldn't . . . not even if I wanted to!" A little lie, perhaps, but ambiguous enough, she concluded.

Pushing his glasses up once more, a habit he resorted to, Cynthia noted, only when he was uncomfortable in a situation, he forced a smile. "Well, I'll give you the address, should you change your mind. I've got work to do on my book, anyway, so I suppose I could use the quiet time, too." Once again there was the ready acceptance and resignation that so characterized Geoffrey's dismal forays into adventure.

At that moment, the waiter appeared with menus, mercifully giving them something more neutral to consider. The rest of the evening was more pleasant, the wine doing its share, as well as the veal, and the world of English literature taking up any remaining slack. It was with genuine fondness that Cynthia hugged him and offered her cheek for a kiss as they bade each other "good night," having made a date to work together at the library on Sunday. No further mention of coordinating their summer vacations was made, as each became swallowed up in the end-of-semester maelstrom.

The next ten days flew by for Cynthia, one blending into the next at the wee hours of the morning when, exhausted and stiff, she arose from the desk to collapse on her bed for several hours of sleep before the alarm jarred her into motion once again. She saw Geoffrey several times during that period, but each was preoccupied with his own work load to the exclusion of most personal chitchat. Much to Cynthia's relief, he was even brief about handing her his address in Vermont, and there was no further appeal for her company other than the noncommital, "Should you change your mind . . ."

Commencement exercises went as planned on the twenty-fourth, and Cynthia, properly attired in cap and gown, joined the other faculty members in the procession, her smile of relief matching theirs, and the dark circles under her eyes the only sign of the strain of the past few weeks. When the festivities were over, she returned to her apartment and slept round the clock, the first time she had ever done so in her life. It was at that moment, when she awoke in a stupor to gaze at the clock and wonder whether it was night or day, then which night or which day, that she saw the wisdom in William Thorpe's words. She really did have to slow down some; this summer would be good for her!

She met her uncle for dinner several days after commencement, and, as always, it was a joy spending time with him. She had taken special pains in dressing for their "date," wishing both to make him proud of her and to convince him that she was thriving personally. As she caught her reflection in the mirror at the front of the restaurant, while she awaited the maitre d', she felt pleased with her efforts. The lavender silk shirt dress, with its low-buttoned neckline opening to a deep vee, its wide sashing at the waist, and the slight fullness below, brought out her slimness, while suggesting just the right amount of femininity. She had applied her makeup as carefully, with a dab of lavender above her outlined eyes, a smudge of rouge on her normally pale cheeks, and a light shade of pink glistening on her lips. Hmm, she mused, glancing as subtly as possible at herself, for a plain girl that's not so bad!

For, although Cynthia Blake knew she could hold her own intellectually, she had never considered her looks to match up. Although quick to acknowledge that she had no truly bad features, her inherent modesty forbade her from recognizing her stronger ones, which had become even more so with age. Her dark brown hair, straight and lustrously healthy, was cut to shoulder length with bangs on the forehead perfectly framing her oval face. She was tall, nearly five feet seven inches, and willowy, with slim hips, a tiny waist, and a fair bustline. Her complexion was clear though pale, her dark brown eyes rounded in their hollows, her nose pert and turned up at the tip, with lips soft and sensuous, feminizing the overall visage. It was when she was all put together, with a smile on that face, that her whole appearance excelled, as it did now with Uncle William approaching her.

"You look wonderful, Cindy! Something must be agreeing with you!" he roared good-heartedly, as he enveloped her in a bear hug before escorting her to their table. "Perhaps a little tired, though," he murmured, as he took a last searching look before seating her and regaining his own seat opposite.

She laughed. "Foiled again! You see too much, Uncle William," she protested, realizing that no amount of concealer could erase the fatigue from her eyes. "Actually, now that school is done for the season, I'm madly trying to compile all of my notes so that I can take off next week for Maine." She sobered in sudden trepidation. "It's all set, isn't it?"

He patted her hand reassuringly. "Yes, it's all set." Then, sitting straighter, he reached into the pocket of his finely tailored jacket and withdrew a thick white envelope, addressed to her, care of her uncle. "Here is all the information you need. There is a lease in there for your use of the cottage over the summer. I've looked it over—didn't think you'd mind—and everything seems in order. All you have to do is sign it and mail it, then get yourself on up there!"

Cynthia took the envelope, raised an eyebrow and regarded her uncle suspiciously. "Professor C. Blake? You didn't tell him? You're a rogue, Uncle William!" she kidded him. Then her gaze swung back to the envelope's upper left-hand corner. "L. Jonathan Roaman . . . is that the 'old miser' we're dealing with?" she laughed, although duly impressed with the Manhattan address of her summer landlord.

William cleared his throat, a sure sign to Cynthia of some gem to come. "Er, he may not be the 'old miser' we have imagined. After all, I wouldn't send you off into the wilds without checking up on your primary link with civilization . . ."

Cynthia's eyes rounded in curiosity. "And . . ."

"It seems your L. Jonathan Roaman is quite the businessman, having built Roaman Enterprises into a multimillion-dollar affair. And—sorry to disappoint you, my dear—he is quite the philanthropist. It appears that he not only gives huge grants each year to various charities, but his factories donate equipment galore to assorted causes."

"With the appropriate tax deductions taken, I'm sure!" she interrupted cynically.

"That I wouldn't know about, but cancer research, for one, has greatly benefited from the generosity of L. Jonathan Roaman," he finished, having made his point before the jury and retiring to await its decision.

"Sounds very noble of him," she conceded, albeit reluctantly. "Well, this is really none of my affair, because I doubt I'll have much to do with him anyway. I intend to make the most of my solitude and play the hermit role to the hilt!"

"Don't go overboard, my dear. Try to have some fun while you're there, or I'll never forgive myself for suggesting it!"

Dear Uncle William, Cynthia reflected, her eyes catching the devotion in his. As he perused the menu, she studied his round face, edged by a thin cap of gray hair, his ruddy complexion and more than double chin a giveaway of his greatest weaknesses in life, food and drink. Despite his size, above average both in height and width, he dressed impeccably, never wearing badly those pounds which he could so easily afford to shed.

Her relationship with him was strong, better than most people have with their own parents. But then, perhaps it was because he was *not* her parent that they were able to keep a certain objectivity with regard to each other. How lucky she was to have him! Smiling warmly as his eyes met hers, she turned her attention to the meal and an evening of lively, relaxed conversation.

It was only later that night, after she had made the proper farewells to him, with a hug and a promise to write regularly, that she thought again of the white envelope which contained the lease and her traveling instructions. She had buried it in her pocketbook at dinner and now, after parking her car in its allotted space and dashing up to her apartment, she eagerly drew it out to learn something more about this Shangri-la she was about to visit.

CHAPTER TWO

"Magnificent" was putting it mildly, Cynthia marveled, as the mail boat departed, leaving her standing, luggage in a neat stack beside her, on the pier at Three Pines. The boat had had no trouble circling the island to the ocean side, where the pier was, before proceeding with its regular mail delivery to Isle au Haut, some three miles off and barely visible in the light midmorning haze. From where she stood, the mainland was out of sight, as though in another world far beyond the rise of the wooded landscape facing her.

To her right swelled a rocky headland, broken and rugged, its boulders strewn like pebbles at the foot of a looming granite precipice. To her left, a more gentle slope stretched to the sea, its upper reaches overspread with low growing junipers, wild rose bushes, and vegetation whose growth still carried the newness of the annual spring revival. The soft grasses and wild flowers at its lower levels magically dissolved into a sand-smooth beach, lapped rhythmically by the incoming tide.

As breathtaking as were these peripheral vistas which ringed the island's core, even more impressive to Cynthia was the dense growth of majestic greenery straight ahead and up, as the island rose one hundred feet or so from the shore into a forest of spruce, balsam, and hemlock. At the island's apex stood three huge pine trees, aged though regal, presiding over nature's dominion as they gave the island her name.

Cynthia felt herself gazing upon a well-planned canvas, whose colors were appropriately chosen, from the somber gray of the lichen-covered rocks to the rich greenness of the firs, enhanced by the silver shoot of an occasional birch, to the multicolored gaiety of the spring wildflowers, their pinks, yellows, and pale blues hovering delicately above the golden sand.

Her eye was drawn to two blinking panels, one directly ahead and about halfway up the mild incline, the other a shadow of the first, smaller, further down, and at that point where the crowd of evergreens yielded to lower growing plant life. It took but a minute to identify the two houses, each with huge panes of glass gaping at the sea from every side. It was toward the larger of the two that Cynthia's gaze riveted, caught by a faint movement among the trees nearby. As she sought its source, a figure emerged from the wooded slope, its form as majestic as the stately pines that towered above.

The man who approached her was tall and lean, his body tapering from broad shoulders to slim hips. He wore white slacks and a red knit shirt, contrasting sharply in color from the greenery elsewhere. Cynthia was most struck as he walked, still some distance from the pier, by his gait, which exuded a supreme confidence and aggressiveness that immobilized her by comparison. As he drew closer, she made out sandy-brown hair, streaked by the sun, and a likewise tawny coloring of the skin.

The stranger's approach mesmerized her, as had the beauty of the island. There was no doubt in her mind, as he drew up to face her, that he was one of the most attractive men she had ever seen. Neither was there any doubt in her mind as to his identity; with a carriage such as he had just demonstrated, he could be none other than the owner of the island, L. Jonathan Roaman.

In her state of utter amazement at this deduction, she found herself staring up into eyes which, although protected from the glare of the sun and its equally potent reflection on the water by a pair of dark sunglasses, shimmered their dazzling blue into her own brown orbs.

"May I help you?" he demanded, his deeply flowing tone sending a shiver through her and snapping her out of her trance.

"I'm looking for an L. Jonathan Roaman," she began somewhat timidly. "You must be he?"

"What is your name?" he shot back curtly, ignoring her question.

"Cynthia Blake . . . Professor Blake. Are you Mr. Roaman?" she repeated, an uneasy feeling taking root at the pit of her stomach as, isolated from help should she need it, she faced this compelling man, who seemed reluctant to disclose his identity.

He continued to stare at her through the dark glasses, his gaze penetrating nonetheless. A puzzled look crossed his features briefly, a fleeting dent in his confidence, before he responded with the smoothness she would have expected.

"Yes. I'm Jonathan Roaman." He paused, a smirk of understanding preceding his next words. "So you're Professor C. Blake?" he asked, with the emphasis on the C, and to her nod he added, "Not quite what I expected!"

"Neither are you!" she returned forcefully, immediately regretting her outburst as he grew more serious. How could she tell him that she had expected an older, more sedentary man, rather than this distractingly masculine person, apparently in his late thirties, whose energy and spirit flowed freely. At least her fear abated somewhat in

28

recalling the good words her uncle had said about this same man. Hurriedly she went on, "I assume that you expected a man?"

"You might say that," he drawled, flashing a heart-stopping smile at her, "though in some respects this could have been a promising development."

At his qualifying remark it was her turn to be puzzled. "I'm not sure I follow . . . what do you mean 'could have been'?" Her words hit his back as he moved toward the end of the pier. Reaching down to the underside of the planking, he withdrew a large red flag on a pole, which he inserted into a close-fitting holder at the tip of the pier. "What's that for?" she asked quickly, beginning to sense what was in his mind.

"The flag will hail the mail boat on its return trip from Isle au Haut." He searched the horizon for any sign of the boat as it headed toward the faint outline of the other island, but it had already passed the point of visibility. "You can get on then and return to the mainland."

Infuriated, Cynthia forgot all hesitancy before this imposing figure. "Wait just a minute! I didn't drive all day yesterday and this morning for a round-trip cruise on some mail boat. I have a lease in my bag which gives me the right to live in that cottage," she pointed emphatically at the smaller of the two, praying that she had made the right assumption, "for three months. You have my money order to prove it. Now, if you'll excuse me, I'm tired and would like to get settled before I collapse." Her momentum continued to gain as she struck one further blow. "If you would be so good as to help me with my things, I can do this in one trip. If not, I'll make two." She had tilted her chin defiantly as she addressed this man who, she was sure, was unused to such aggressiveness. He was most likely, she seethed inwardly, the type who demanded obedience from all his subjects. Well, she was not one of his typical subjects, and the sooner he realized that, the

29

better, she reasoned. As she bent to pick up the first of her bags, she heard the sound of applause behind her. She straightened and turned slowly toward him, hands on her hips, to await his elaboration.

The broad grin that lit up his rugged features disarmed her, causing her embarrassment at her sudden outburst. She was usually so patient, she chided herself, that it had to be either her own fatigue, or the odd effect that this stranger had on her . . . and the thought of the latter perplexed her all the more.

Jonathan stopped clapping to gaze down at her mockingly. "You've been listening to too many of Attorney Thorpe's final arguments! Or do you lecture to your classes that way, Professor Blake?"

"The name is Cynthia, and William Thorpe is my uncle. It was he who suggested that I come here, and he said nothing about my gender being improper," she retorted angrily.

"Oh, there certainly *is* nothing improper about your gender. In fact, it's quite commendable . . ." His voice trailed off, as his eyes, glittering strongly through their dark shades, moved slowly down the length of her body, before returning to her face, now a faint pink under the impact of his scrutiny. He continued, more gently, "It's just that there is a job to be done here, and a man would be better suited for it."

"In what way?" she shot back, again raising her chin in defiance. Although the times were such that a woman often had an easier time getting a job under the guise of sexual equality, Cynthia knew that there would always remain some bastions of male chauvinism. Militant she was not, yet she would never back down from a good intellectual attempt to corner one of the offenders.

He had grown quite serious again. "What do you know of this job, Cynthia? What did your uncle tell you?"

"I was told you needed someone to stay on the island,

to keep watch for anything amiss while you were not here," she stated matter-of-factly.

"And what did your pretty little head tell you to be on the lookout for?" he taunted, with no humor in his words.

"Ah, I don't really know . . . fire . . . burst water pipes . . . that kind of thing, I suppose," she replied, experiencing the same unease she had felt when the proposal had been first put to her nearly a month ago. "What had *you* had in mind?" she cornered him, aiming to free herself from the hot seat.

She returned his intent gaze, reluctantly admiring at close range his startling good looks. There was a rakish quality about his face, his forehead hidden by the thickness of his sandy hair, his nose fine and straight, except at one point where the slightest crook had been put in, no doubt, she mused, in some game of touch football at prep school, and his jaw squared beneath the trace of a five-o'clock shadow which, at eleven o'clock in the morning, had stubbornly made its appearance.

He didn't speak, apparently lost in his own thoughts as he assimilated her features with the same thoroughness. It occurred to Cynthia that he was planning his approach, carefully deciding what he wanted to say, and the sense of mystery heightened the excitement which his presence created within her.

Slowly he began. "There's been some trouble lately with trespassers on these islands . . ." He hesitated again. "Day trippers . . . they seem to feel that this is a perfect spot, out of sight of the mainland, to have their fun." He continued more readily, as though he now knew what he would tell her. "This is a privately owned island. I will not be cleaning up after tourists, and I don't like the idea of anyone breaking into my homes. So, you see, what I wanted was something more like a watchdog . . ." Again his gaze swept over her judgmentally. "What would you do if the island was invaded?"

31

"I should think the idea of my being here would be enough to deter most trespassers," she answered, trying to sound convinced herself.

"But what if, for example, a cruiser with four rowdy gentlemen aboard tied up at the pier and the men ceased both to be aboard and to be gentlemen, how would you defend yourself, let alone my island?" His eyebrow raised in a suggestion of wit, though his lingering sobriety sent a chill through her.

"I don't know karate, if that's what you are asking. Nor do I carry a gun," she answered scornfully. "But I've been able to avoid rape so far!"

His satanic smile sent a chill of a very different kind through her. For the first time, she noticed a faint scar on his jawline, which added to his roguish air.

"That's what I was . . . afraid of," he drawled, his implication clear as his gaze lowered from her face to her breasts, their gentle fullness evident through the soft terry material of the sweatshirt she had worn with her jeans. Never before had a man's gaze affected her as his did, her every nerve end clamoring at his visual caress, her breasts growing fuller under his very eye.

Dismayed by these involuntary reactions of her body, Cynthia became angry, more at herself than at him, although he had no way of knowing that. "It seems that you may be more of a danger than some wandering sailors! Do you make it a habit to look at women that way?" she demanded.

"Only when they are as beautifully belligerent as you are! What are you doing all alone up here for the summer? I would think you'd have a whole entourage on your tail," he smiled, warmly this time, with no hint of the mockery that she would have expected. Although she refused to take his sideways compliment seriously, it melted her anger instantly.

"Not quite. I've got to work. My dissertation needs the

32

peace and solitude of a place like this. And that's why I'm staying," she avowed, as she stalked past him, removed the red flag from its holster, and replaced it under the pier, in doing so demonstrating her ability to catch onto where and how things worked. "Now, I'd really like to unpack . . . if you'd be so kind," she concluded, passing him again—a look on his face of mild amazement at her determination, she noted with satisfaction—as she leaned over to get her luggage.

Jonathan Roaman was not one to be put off so easily though; she found herself being twirled around to face him, powerful hands around her upper arms effectively immobilizing her. His tone, when he finally spoke, was neither angry nor disrespectful, but rather one of caution and warning. "Let's get one thing straight, Cynthia. You may be perfectly adept at taking care of yourself, but never forget that this is my island and you are therefore my responsibility. If I feel that there's any danger, you'll do as I say. Understood?" His grip tightened, indicating that there would be no release until she complied.

But she was not yet ready to cower before him. Forcing herself to ignore the pain in her arms from his bruising grasp, she tilted her chin up and spoke back to him. "If you have some demand to make, Mr. Roaman, the least you could do is to come out from behind those glasses and give your orders directly." It had been an impulsive request on her part and she was as perplexed with her behavior as he was.

Releasing one arm, Jonathan reached up and slowly, deliberately, removed his sunglasses. Instantly Cynthia regretted her suggestion, for the shimmering blueness of his eyes seared into her with a fierceness which deprived her of purpose and sent a bolt through her veins. If she had been taken with this man's looks before, she was now totally overwhelmed, as she tried desperately to maintain her poise and prevent him from seeing the toll his nearness was taking on her.

No word was spoken as the brilliance of his gaze explored her face, tenderly skimming her cheeks, sensuously tracing her jaw from ear to chin, softly coming to a rest on her lips, which parted involuntarily at his caress. So deeply was she entranced that she had to fight her way upward from the depths to hear, now gently spoken, the repetition of his demand.

"Understood?"

She raised her own gaze from the allure of lips, which had murmured so seductively, to his eyes, and managed a breathless, "Yes," before mustering every ounce of remaining resistance to pull her arm free of his grasp and turn away from him, thus breaking the spell he had cast over her.

Shaken to the core, she reached for her luggage forcefully, anxious to clasp the handles which would still the trembling in her hands. She then began to walk up the pier and across the sand toward the path which led to the cottage she assumed to be hers. She didn't spare a backward glance, though she was soon able to hear footsteps following her in silent acknowledgment that her surmise had been correct.

The walk was not long, but Cynthia's muscles rebelled as the door of the cottage came into view. The trembling had abated but left in its wake a numbness which tired her all the more. As she put her luggage down before the door, a firm hand reached around her and grasped the handle, turning it to give Cynthia leeway to enter the most charming, if modern structures can muster charm, one-room cabin she had ever seen.

Pentagonal in shape, the three sides facing the ocean were glass enclosed, the other two sides paneled in a natural white pine, rough-hewn and rustic. The ceiling rose to a point in its center, skylights scattered liberally around its rim. The furnishing was strictly functional, with bunks, built into the three sides below the glass panels, doubling as sofas with their magnificent view of the water. The two paneled walls bore strategically placed built-ins offering kitchen facilities and a breakfast bar, with cabinets and shelves above for storage. There were several lush-pile rugs on the planked floor, two low coffee tables, and a small dining table near the kitchen. Other than the front door, in which she now stood, only one other door was evident, leading into what Cynthia assumed to be the bathroom.

"Does it meet with your approval?" the deep voice at her ear asked, innocent enough.

Cynthia bounded forward, shocked by its unexpected nearness . . . and reluctant to have a repetition of her earlier, and in her mind appalling, enrapture by his charm. "Fantastic!" she exclaimed breathlessly, praying that her wispy tone was due either to the walk up or the appeal of the cottage, rather than her eminently masculine landlord.

Jonathan walked toward the windows, put her bags on the bed, and then turned to her. "I think you'll find everything you need. There are already some supplies in the kitchen, but if you make a list of whatever else you want, I would be glad to pick them up for you. I'll be going into Stonington later this afternoon. If you'd like, you can come." His tone was smooth and pleasant, apparently undisturbed by any of the factors that may have affected her own.

"Thank you, but I'm really exhausted. It's been a long semester and a long trip," she explained, looking toward the pier to avoid his eyes. "How do you get in to the village? I didn't see any boat." She approached the window as she spoke, staring down at the empty pier.

"Very observant . . . chalk one for you!" he teased softly. "My boat has been on the mainland all week for repairs, or I would have picked you up myself . . . had I known . . ." Cynthia shot an annoyed glance back at

35

him, knowing only too well to what he referred. "A friend is bringing it out to me. Then I'll drop him back at the village. I'll be going at about five o'clock, so you have plenty of time to see what you need."

Cynthia turned back to thank him and escort him out of the house. Scrutinizing her face, he seemed concerned. "You look pale. Are you all right?"

Beginning to feel particularly weak at this point, she nodded. "I'm just tired. I could really use some sleep. But I will make a grocery list before I pass out," she cracked, smiling tentatively.

His view shifted toward one of the beds, as he drawled intimately, "Make sure you get yourself properly settled first," and his smile bedazzled her a final time before he turned, left the cabin, and disappeared up the path toward the larger house.

Saturday

Dear Uncle William,

Just a line to tell you that I arrived on Three Pines this morning, safe and sound. You were right—it was a very long and tiring trip. At several points I regretted not taking your advice and traveling by bus, though I do feel much better knowing that I have my own car garaged in the village and will thus have greater flexibility when I want to go to the library.

Mr. Roaman's directions were perfect. After leaving Philly yesterday morning, I drove straight through New York, Connecticut, and Massachusetts. Spent the night at a dumpy little motel in Portsmouth which served a great cup of chowder in its coffee shop, and I was on my way first thing this morning.

Yes, I agree with you. The Maine Turnpike does get monotonous after thirty or forty miles of super-highway. Not quite up to my expectations—until I reached Augusta and left the turnpike. One town surpassed the next in charm—Belfast, Castine, Brooksville. It was as though the pace slowed from one to the next, the further I got from the highway.

The towns are delightful! I stopped for breakfast at a little restaurant in Castine. I was the only "stranger" there. As for everyone else, they could have been in their own kitchens for the easy conversation and utter familiarity with each other. When I asked for a menu, it was as if the waitress had to stop to remember where she might have left it last month!

Stonington is the further of the two towns on Deer Isle. The place is terrific—quaint and friendly. I had no problem making arrangements with Mr. Bailey, the owner of the hardware store, to garage my car behind his home. You should see his store—it's more like a general store or a department store! And he, too, seemed to know everyone on a first-name basis. Quite a switch for this little girl from the inner city!

As Mr. Roaman had outlined, the driver of the mail boat was more than happy to drop me here on the island, even though it was slightly out of the way of his normal weaving route through the harbor islands. I got the same feeling from him as I did from Mr. Bailey and the others I've seen here: Time can fly as fast as it wants, but they will take their pleasant time about living, enjoying every routine and every diversion. Don't you admire their attitude, Uncle William? If only it were contagious, I'd return to Philly next fall a much, much more relaxed person!

Mr. Roaman met me here and showed me to my cottage. It is contemporary in design and fully equipped with all of the modern conveniences, though it blends exquisitely with the character of the island.

I've done most of my unpacking, although my typewriter will remain strategically hidden under a bed for several days until I catch up on my rest. It was so good of you to suggest my coming here, Uncle William! Thank you!

Let me close now so that I can get this letter to Mr. Roaman to mail when he goes to the mainland later today. I'll be thinking of you as I bask in the sun on my own private down east Waikiki! Take care!

Your loving niece,
Cynthia

Folding the letter, Cynthia addressed, sealed, and stamped its envelope before placing it on the table with her grocery list. Turning, she approached the window, sinking onto one of the beds to gaze out over the ocean. The movement of the water hypnotized her, sparkles of sunlight dancing back and forth over the blue-gray depths. The sound of its heartbeat was strong, the regular pounding of the waves against the beach penetrating the Thermopane and lulling her with its rhythm.

As she thought fondly of Uncle William and the letter she had just written, it occurred to her that she had, subconsciously or otherwise, avoided description of the two most important though somewhat disturbing elements of her trip so far: her "job" and Jonathan Roaman. The former strangely puzzled her, for she had gotten the distinct feeling that Jonathan was being dramatic in his suggestion of vandalism, destruction and, indeed, rape; that he did not really anticipate such occurrences. Surely, if he were genuinely concerned, he would have gates, guard dogs, or alarm systems, any of which he could only too well afford. But rather he had hired, blindly at that—although evidently he thought as highly of John Cummings as Cummings thought of her uncle—someone to keep an eye on things. He hadn't even given her much of an argument when she showed her determination to stay on the island. His was merely a token attempt to scare her away, as though he hadn't really wanted to do that.

Well, it hadn't worked and she was staying . . . and she would certainly keep a lookout for any trespassers. Not that they could do her more harm than Jonathan Roaman himself . . .

Why hadn't she mentioned more about Jonathan to Uncle William, she asked herself. Was it because there wasn't that much to say? She knew better than that. Was it because her uncle wouldn't have been interested? She doubted that, because he had always been genuinely concerned about what she did and with whom she spent her time. Rather, she suspected it was because she would have been totally unable to describe Jonathan in the objective words which were appropriate to use about a man whom she had known for a mere thirty minutes!

Would she tell her uncle that Jonathan was beyond a doubt the most handsome man she had ever met? Should she tell her uncle that Jonathan had been surprised, though not unpleasantly so, at Professor Blake's turning out to be a woman? Could she tell him that, in their brief meeting, Jonathan moved something within her that no man in her life had ever done before, that his nearness aroused feelings, involuntary yet demanding, which perplexed and frightened her even as they excited her?

How could she write about these things that she didn't understand herself? No, she would have to wait until her feelings sorted themselves out before she could share them, even with someone as dear to her as her uncle.

Suddenly, the pulsating beat of the surf became too much for Cynthia's tired body. Covering herself with the large knit afghan she had found in one of the storage drawers under the bed during her thorough exploration of the cabin earlier, she immediately drifted off into a deep sleep, the sounds of the sea a perpetual lullaby, the cradle of the waves rocking back and forth against rocks and sand.

When she awoke it was nearly dark, the sun having fallen well below the level of the three pines, casting the island's own shadow on the beach, the boulders, and the pier below. Only the orange and red highlights on the whitecaps further to the east were a reminder of what had been and would no doubt be again. Even these lines of color were fading fast before Cynthia's eyes, the blue-purple aura of dusk replacing the last vestiges of day.

Her list! The letter! With a jolt, Cynthia realized that she must have slept for hours and would have missed catching Jonathan before he left for the mainland. There was no sign of a boat at the pier. Neither was there any sign, as she looked toward the table, of her letter or the grocery list! Chagrined, she understood instinctively that Jonathan had come in while she slept and had taken the two items. Arrogant as he was, he would not be one to stand on ceremony when his knock, had there indeed been one, went unanswered, she concluded angrily.

Trying to plot things out rationally, Cynthia deduced that because her letter and list were gone, Jonathan must have left earlier for the mainland—her watch told her it was almost eight o'clock—but that, because there was no sign of the boat, he had not returned yet. Therefore, she had little recourse but to stay put until he did. She had not been up to his cabin in daylight and did not dare try to reach it now in the dim, prelunar evening.

There had actually been a fair number of supplies stacked in the kitchen cabinets when she had arrived. From these, she managed to prepare herself a delightful dinner, which she then ate in style, lit by the dim glow of a hurricane lamp and serenaded by the song of the sea. She felt so much fresher, having slept off some of the wear of the journey, and revived following her meal, that she sat back for a while, ingesting the smells and sounds of her new, albeit temporary, home.

The air was clear, the smell that touched her senses an intermingling of sharp resin and salt spray. If only she could bottle this scent and have it with her always! As she sat, alone and in silence, she felt a certain peace which she hadn't felt for a long, long time. It was the summer of her ninth year when her parents had taken her to the mountains. She had wandered off from their cabin to a small pine grove, the smell of the needles even now floating back to her. Sitting there on a cushion of fallen leaves so many years ago, she had experienced the same oneness with nature, the same inner tranquility that she felt now. Of course, she rued, it was always shattered by the inevitable return to civilization.

Chilly as the late spring night air was, Cynthia had opened one of the huge windows slightly to bring her even closer to the nocturnal life of the island. Above the slap and slur of the gently rolling tide, there was the occasional sound of a mosquito, attracted by her light, dashing itself against the screen.

As she looked past these misguided insects out across the ocean once again, a steadily moving light, or group of lights, she realized upon closer inspection, caught her eye. She was fascinated by its movement, smooth and even over the water, the lap of the tide against its painted hull a delightful addition to the evening symphony. It was with momentary trepidation that she saw the craft glide alongside the pier—was this Jonathan or an unwelcome visitor? But her fears were put to rest by the loud clang of the boat's bell, announcing its arrival. Such boldness, she smiled, would come from none other than her self-sure island-owner.

Grabbing the large torch flashlight that had hung on the wall beside the sink, she left the cabin and lighted her way

41

down the narrow pathway, retracing her steps of the morning to the pier.

Jonathan must have seen her beam winding its way down the hillside, for he was not in the least surprised to look up, from where he was busily tying the boat to the pier, and see her approaching him. The lights from the yacht cast a dim glow over all in its radius, and Cynthia couldn't help but admire anew Jonathan's good looks. He wore navy slacks and a matching blazer, its brass buttons twinkling in reflection of the other lights. His white cotton shirt gave a crispness to the image, all of which her mind assimilated. But, much to her dismay, she found her eyes straying toward his neck and chest, where his shirt lay open to reveal sandy wisps on a bronzed base, his muscles straining against the material as he buried his hands in his pants pockets, thus minimizing the blazer's coverage.

"Hi, sleepyhead!" he greeted her, his open smile displaying teeth as white as his shirt. "You were dead to the world. A fine watchdog you're going to make! Anyone could walk in and do who-knows-what, and you'd sleeep through it all!" Cynthia's mouth opened in silent protest, but he went on, "Feeling better?" His friendliness seemed sincere enough. As much as she tried, she could not be angry at his subtle accusation; neither could she begrudge him his foray into her living quarters earlier, especially as the dimness of the evening mercifully hid from his gaze the faint blush that had crept onto her cheeks.

"Much," she replied enthusiastically. "I'm sorry I missed you. Thanks for mailing my letter. Was it much trouble picking up the things I listed?"

He shook his head valiantly. "Not at all! I handed the list to Mr. Ellis and he filled the order. Simple as that . . . and charged to your account. You can even up with him at the end of the month." He was in a particularly good mood, Cynthia reflected. Had he actually been pleased to see her, or was it her own imagination, spurred on by the jumping in her stomach, that played tricks on her? She wasn't going to waste time wondering, as she forced her attention to the yacht which was now secured safely.

"The boat is beautiful! Is it all fixed?" she asked, her eye skimming the bow of the late model, newly painted and polished, its registration number in bold form. The craft measured at least thirty feet, she estimated, from bow to stern, though she was unable to see the latter from her vantage point on the pier and would have been hesitant to push Jonathan into a grand tour.

Leaning forward to adjust one of the floats that padded the boat from the beating of the dock, he smiled proudly. "Yes, ma'am. She is a beauty, isn't she?" It was evident to Cynthia that boating, indeed the ocean itself, was a joy to Jonathan. For only a person who appreciated the sea's raw beauty would have built a home as he had, walls decorated for all times with the ever-changing, ever-constant animation of the currents. Only a person who adored the sea would isolate himself from the civilized world as Jonathan had, at the mercy of the naked fury which her waters could summon, dependent on this one sleek craft to bind him to his fellow man.

"How long have you owned her?"

"Three years now. I enjoy the yacht almost as much as I do the island," he explained, grinning sheepishly in an endearingly boyish way.

Her reply was in earnest. "I can see that." Her tone held no derision and he seemed buoyed up by it, although he still made no move to invite her aboard.

Instead, he turned his piercing blue gaze on her for a moment—an eternal moment of exquisite torture for Cynthia, whose nerves tingled madly under his sensual eye—before he spoke, quietly and gently, his low tone as arousing as his gaze had been.

"I'll take you for a cruise next week. We can make a

day of it, through the islands. Say Thursday . . . can you take the time off?"

"From my work or yours?" she countered, stalling for time, trying not to sound over-eager, knowing all the while that she would not, could not refuse his invitation. Funny, though, she noted, his had been more of a statement of intention than a request.

Sensing her hesitancy, he moved closer and reached out to put one hand gently, reassuringly on her shoulder. His back was to the boat, but the moon had risen over the three pines and now faintly and suggestively outlined his features, emphasizing the strength of his nose and chin, the purposefulness of his jawline, the invitation of his lips. Most compelling, though, were his eyes, the sparkling moonlight blinking back at Cynthia from their blue crystals. Her heart seemed to stop beating for a minute and then resumed in thunderous reprisal. She felt her mouth go dry and subconsciously touched her lips with her tongue.

"You shouldn't do that, Cynthia," he chided softly, a strange and new huskiness in his voice.

"Do what?" she asked, mesmerized by his nearness and oblivious to all else, the least of which her own provocative gesture.

The same huskiness came through even his whisper. "Oh, hell . . . you weren't supposed to be a woman . . ." His words trailed off as his mouth descended slowly, slowly, drawn to hers like a magnet whose force increases with nearness and whose power overcomes all resistance.

Cynthia heard his words, sensed his initial reluctance, but was as unable as he to divert physical energy from its present course. Her lips parted as his touched them, lightly, experimentally, in a shy and innocent exploration which she returned, its sweetness increasing the craving tenfold. It was a kiss of pure feeling, the joy of one moment becoming the impetus of the next.

Their lips finally parted in mutual separation, a necessary breather for each. But the flame had already been kindled; there was no turning back. As they stood gazing at each other, Cynthia caught her breath sharply, her heart thudding loudly in her chest. She had never been caught up like this; the passionate longings of her body for this man's touch startled her. She knew that she had lost control, her body reacting instinctively to Jonathan, when she eagerly moved to meet him. His head lowered once again and his lips possessed hers, this time with an intensity which surpassed all but that of her own responding lips.

As his arms circled her, drawing her against the muscular lines of his torso, her hands spread over his chest, moving caressingly to his shoulders, powerful and broad, before meeting at the nape of his neck. The kiss deepened now, his tongue seeking hers, its touch sending vibrations through her entire being, igniting a separate fire, fierce and unexpected, in her loins. It was the similar response in his body, which she felt quite distinctly, that gave her the momentary strength to withdraw from his embrace.

They stood thus, in silence, mere inches from each other, their bodies apart yet his hands remaining on her waist as hers remained on his shoulders. The moon, to give them privacy, had disappeared behind a passing cloud, and Cynthia could no longer read his expression. Only the irregularity of his breathing gave testimony to his arousal moments before—or was it her own pulse that echoed so deafeningly in her ears?

He didn't move any closer, but raised a thumb to caress her lips as he whispered, "Then you'll join me on Thursday?"

She didn't trust her voice, his touch so seductively near; she merely nodded in acceptance, her eyes not leaving his face for a minute.

"Good," he murmured, then paused, and, in the face of some private dilemma, yielded to a pregnant silence. Suddenly he tensed—had Cynthia heard the same noise from the boat that he had—and, releasing her he turned and called over his shoulder, "I'll get your groceries," as he walked toward the cabin and disappeared from sight.

Cynthia felt devastated, both by the loss of his warmth and by her own unfulfilled desires. She knew too well the turmoil of her own emotions, but his were an enigma to her. As ardent as was his embrace, she sensed there had been a certain reluctance in his excitement. What thoughts possessed that magnificent mind, she wondered. What was the mystery, so faint yet omnipresent? Her instinct told her that this man was attracted to her, yet she couldn't help but shiver at the undercurrent of tension which played hide-and-seek with his responses to her.

Of one thing she was all too sure: Jonathan Roaman captivated her, mind and body, as no man had ever done. Her hardest job this summer, she feared, would be to hide these feelings from him, at least until she resolved the quandary that so unsettled her. Little did she know that she was about to be confronted by the one piece that would prove hardest to fit into the puzzle.

CHAPTER THREE

Jonathan was gone for no more than a minute before he reemerged from the cabin carrying the large brown bag that contained her supplies. Stepping forward to relieve him of his burden, she drew even with the porthole on the pier side of the cabin. A movement caught her eye and she skirted him to take a closer look. What she saw froze blood that had so recently flowed hot with passion. Through eyes wide with shock, she caught the swirl of red chiffon, the flow of blonde hair, the unmistakably voluptuous curves . . . and then she saw no more as she turned, snatched her parcel from Jonathan wordlessly, and ran up the pier to the path, her hand white-knuckled with tension as it held the torch to light her way up the darkened hillside to her cottage.

It was only when she had closed the door behind her and fastened the latch, which she had mistakenly ignored earlier in the day, that she gave way to the tears of anger and hurt which had gathered during her retreat. What kind of monster could this man be? How could he have embraced her so tenderly right there on the dock, but a few feet from the boat in which his girlfriend was tidying up after a candlelight dinner? How could he have used her so? What was he trying to prove? What kind of unfeeling being was he?

She slid down to the floor, her back against the door, the grocery bag still in her arms. Only the dim light of the lamp lit the room with its orange glow. The tears slowed, then dried on her cheeks as her mind raced round and round the many questions that she asked. The mystery had deepened; the shadow of reluctance had taken shape . . . quite definitely. So that was why he had held back. And she had been fool enough to succumb to his virility! Clasping her stomach as she remembered her own reckless behavior, shame overwhelmed her.

She felt, more than heard, the soft tapping on the door behind her. Why had he followed her here? Was he that callous? Again, the knock. She neither moved nor spoke. The silence was ear-splitting. This time, the rap was louder, firm knuckles against firmer wood. She remained unresponding, paralyzed by her emotions. It was the sound of his voice—was that concern in his tone or merly impatience—which snapped her out of her stupor?

"Cynthia . . . open the door!" He waited, then tried again. "Open up, Cynthia. I have to see you."

Her response was hesitant at first, then gaining in determination. "I'm going to bed now, Mr. Roaman," she lied. "Would you please leave!"

She was unprepared for his vehemence. "No, I won't leave. Not until you open the door. Come on, Cynthia. I'll break it down if I have to . . ."

She knew he was serious and feared, recalling the strength in the arms and shoulders which had held her, that he would have no trouble carrying out his threat.

"Cynthia . . ." His tone was menacing now. Slowly, she stood up and unbolted the door, opening it the minimum necessary to converse with him. Gathering every drop of composure that remained in her—a paltry bit, she feared—she repeated her earlier words.

"I'd like to go to sleep. Do you mind?"

The force with which he pushed the door open threw her off balance and she stumbled backward, saved from the hard wood floor only by the two sturdy hands that steadied her shoulders. As she stiffened, he dropped his hands to his sides.

"Are you all right?" he asked gently.

Her words reflected the coldness that had begun to spread from her insides out. "I'm fine. Now, would you please leave?"

He stared intently at her face, a sincerity in his eyes that she knew now to be fraudulent. He spoke deliberately, measuring each word. "I wish I could explain to you, Cynthia . . . but I can't!" Well, she rationalized, at least he knew he had a problem!

His hand moved to her cheek to wipe away a lingering tear, but she recoiled from his touch and moved tensely away from him. "There's nothing to explain," she shot back, rising anger giving her strength. "Now, please leave!" She boldly walked around him to the door to reinforce her suggestion.

When he walked to the door, she breathed a quiet sigh of relief. At its threshold, he turned and flashed her the most dazzling of smiles, piercing her shell of anger against her very wishes and touching off an aftershock, a sad imitation, she told herself, of his earlier potency.

He spoke firmly. "My friends call me Jonathan," then he waited for a response.

His had been the trump card earlier; now it was her turn. In her sauciest of tones, she retorted, "That's nice. Now, good night, Mr. Roaman," and she dramatically slammed the door and noisily fastened the bolt. Then she leaned against it once more, listening for any sign of rebuttal from the outside but only hearing the tumultuous beat of her own heart.

The next few days passed peacefully for Cynthia, giving her the chance to put some ever-healing time between herself and her emotions of that Saturday night. To have seesawed from one extreme to the other so abruptly— from the high of the awesome passion shared with Jonathan in one moment, to the low of anger, treachery, and abuse the next! It took a good twenty-four hours for her fists to unclench of their own free will, and from then on she made a slow but steady recovery from the emotional wound.

To her detriment, she was somehow always aware of Jonathan's comings and goings—with walls of glass, how could she miss any major movement on the island? She saw him leave with his date on Sunday morning—why would she have come only for such a short time? Then she saw Jonathan return alone in the golden glimmer of the late afternoon sun. She watched him take an early morning swim on Monday and again on Tuesday; this seemed to be his special time and she made a note to avoid the beach at that hour. On each of these days she saw a lobster boat, old and weathered but strong of motor, pull up to the pier and take Jonathan on in the morning, to return him to the island late in the day.

She buried herself in her work, its demanding concentration freeing her of the brooding that would otherwise have possessed her. Once she realized that Jonathan would be gone for most of the day, she took to swimming, herself, around noontime, for a much needed flexing of her muscles. She even indulged in sunbathing on the short stretch of smooth and soft sandy beach which opened to the Atlantic. It was at these moments, beautiful as they were with the warming rays of the sun recompensing the chill of the ocean and its onshore breeze, that she thought of Jonathan, whose breathtakingly masculine form swam the same waters and lounged on the same beach as she did now.

He was a puzzlement to her. As much as understanding people and their motivations was her very field of expertise, she could make no headway in understanding this one. Of course, she had little to work with—no family background, no information on his business activities, no personal data other than that he was wealthy, charitable, and unbelievably appealing as a man to the opposite sex. She doubted she would ever learn more, because she had already decided not to go with him on Thursday.

On the positive side of this summer experience, she was immensely pleased with the cottage. It was totally functional, thoroughly equipped to satisfy all her needs, and allowed her a communion with nature that she adored. She awoke in the morning with the sun, as it slowly edged over the horizon to the east and cast its glow through her windows. She went to bed at night after its warmth had dissipated in the cool of evening, long orange streaks having faded into the dark and starlit night. And throughout it all were the smells and sounds of the island: the aroma of pine and hemlock, the lingering wafts of wood smoke from the upper cottage, and the ever-present, ever-changing tempo of the tides, lapping rhythmically against the shore.

Additionally, she was beginning to make real progress in her work. The luxury of having eight hours a day of uninterrupted tranquility was something she had sorely missed back in Philadelphia. If the summer progressed as these first few days had, she would be assured of the completion of her dissertation. It was an exciting prospect to Cynthia, one that made her all the more eager to delve into her work each morning.

Thursday morning dawned bright and clear. Cynthia

51

awoke with the first light, and looked down to the beach to see Jonathan's tawny head bobbing a path through the waves, his powerful stroke carrying him out against the current, then in again at double speed before turning to make the swim away from the shore once again. This was the day that could have been so exciting for her . . .

She washed, put on a shirt and jeans, and quickly breakfasted, determined to immerse herself in the pile of papers that would occupy her mind to the exclusion of any wishful thinking which might tempt her. But her escape was not to be so easy.

A hard knock at the door jolted her out of her complacency. Although she had been too busy with her writing to see anyone on the path, she knew who this would be. She also knew that, if her experience the other night was any indication, it would do her no good to ignore his knock.

Lingering in her chair as long as she dared, she arose slowly and walked to the door, mustering as much composure as she hoped would sustain her under his scrutiny. It was barely enough, she rued, as she opened the door to face Jonathan, dashingly handsome in his crisp white shirt, faded denims, and canvas boating shoes. The short sleeves and open neck of his fitted shirt emphasized the evenly bronzed hue of his skin, broken only by the sun-bleached hairs that sprouted provocatively on his arms and chest.

Cynthia strained to keep her eyes on his, resolved that he would get no satisfaction from the admiration to which he was clearly accustomed. In as indifferent a voice as she could produce, given the odds against it, she inquired, "Was there something you wanted, Mr. Roaman?"

He grinned in amusement at her use of the formality. "We had a date. Are you all set to go?" His tone was one of confidence. Her refusal could be difficult to get across . . .

"Oh, I'm sorry. I really can't make it. I just have too much work to do. Thank you anyway." She struggled to

52

keep her manner civil, as anger at his audacity gathered within her. Anxious to conclude the interchange, she made a movement to reclose the door. It was rudely blocked by a forceful arm and leg pushing it open even further as he entered the cabin.

"I think you can leave your work for one day. You've already gotten more done than you expected this week." How had he known, she fumed? Could he be that aware of her activities even when he was off the island?

She persisted. "I'm in the middle of a delicate analysis. If I leave now, I'll lose a lot of time and then have to start it all over again." It was becoming more and more difficult for her to remain patient, in the face of his pressure, multifaceted as it was. For even as he stood before her, she felt the lure of his male attraction, the pure chemistry that drew her toward him.

A look of impatience crossed his own face. "Look . . . it's too beautiful a day to stand arguing. The wind is just right to raise the sails. I'm going down to get the boat ready. Be down in ten minutes." He turned and strode down the path, leaving no time for further dissent.

She shut the door and went to the window where she looked longingly at him and the craft. It really would be fun. And he had been right about her work. But could she trust him? Could she trust herself? Why reopen the wound that was finally healing!

Reluctantly and with grudging determination, she resumed her seat at the table and made a show of taking up her work where she'd left off. It was here that Jonathan found her ten minutes later, having anticipated that she would not join him willingly. He barged into the room—why had she left the bolt undone again?—and glared at her for several seconds, before he went to the closet, rummaged through the clothes that hung there, and, to her consternation, withdrew the heavy sweater-jacket which she had thought to pack at the last minute on the outside chance that she would run into cold weather.

"What do you think you're doing?" she demanded, finally finding her tongue as she stood to confront him.

He made no reply, but stalked toward her and clamped a viselike grip on her arm, just above the elbow, in clear indication that he would personally escort her to the pier.

She struggled to free her arm. "Let go of me! You have no authority over me! I have work to do."

His grip tightened, hurting her intentionally, she was sure. "I do have authority. You are on my property doing a job for me. This is your work for today." He paused, regaining his own composure. "Now . . . do you have anything you want to bring?"

She glared at him, furious at his insolence, incensed by his arrogance. "You're hurting my arm," she said through gritted teeth. "Let . . . me . . . go!" she demanded one final time.

His bruising grip made her wince as he pulled her beside him out of the cabin, slammed the door shut behind them, and led her down the path. She said nothing, wanting to avoid further humiliation. He was vehement in his intention that she accompany him. All she wanted now was relief from the pain in her arm.

His pace did not slacken even when they reached the pier. She protested with as much self-control as she could find. "Please release my arm. It hurts! I won't run away," she added sarcastically. Her plea fell on deaf ears as he wordlessly hustled her aboard the boat and into the cockpit, where he threw her into a chair, her sweater onto her lap, with the cold command, "Sit there while I untie the boat."

Terrified to defy him, she remained where she was, gently rubbing the arm that she knew would show the sign of his abuse for days to come. She felt the boat float slowly away from the pier as Jonathan reentered the cockpit and, without a glance at her, started the engine to take them to open water.

Cynthia watched him as he navigated the yacht, turning it around and heading away from the shore toward the south end of the island. He was a striking figure, standing at the controls, exuding confidence and competence. He was perfectly at ease directing his craft, as he must have done hundreds of times through these waters.

When they had passed the tip of Three Pines, he killed the motor and headed out of the cockpit to raise the sails. Not sure whether she would be permitted to move yet, Cynthia stayed where she was until he turned, on the top step, and addressed her. All trace of anger was gone from his voice—the ocean had already begun its soothing effect—and, if anything, she caught a trace of humor.

"I haven't chained you to that chair. You can move around as you like now."

"Does that include swimming back to the island?" she shot back impulsively, then realized how childish, no—stupid, her words were.

"Sure . . . as long as you don't mind swimming in your clothes. You may meet an occasional shark, but don't let that bother you. You'll be so numb you won't feel a thing, after a few minutes in that water! Want a boost overboard?"

She threw a hateful glance in his direction, but he had escaped topside before it could hit its mark. What nerve the man had, she seethed. To force her to come like this against her will! She'd let him know a thing or two. Indignantly she climbed to the upper deck where Jonathan was busily raising the jib sheet. Before she could open her mouth, he commanded, "Grab this line, will you?"

In any other situation she would have flatly refused to follow his order. But the instant she stepped up on the deck she involuntarily sensed the excitement of the yacht's activity. She moved quickly to take the halyard from him.

As the sails unfurled, the wind instantly captivated them, sending the yacht forward through the gray-blue water. For Cynthia, the feeling was nothing short of exhilarating, as the wind blew against her cheeks, whipping her straight brown hair out behind her. It was a magnificent day for a cruise; as much as she begrudged Jonathan his whim, she felt her anger and tension evaporating, cast to the winds as were the sails billowing above her.

"Nice, isn't it?" Jonathan had somehow sensed her change of mood and indicated as much, as he came to relieve her of the line.

Not yet up to conversation with him, she agreed simply, "Mmmm . . .", as she closed her eyes and turned her face to the sun to bask in its warmth.

"Are you too cool?" he inquired, noticing that she had left her sweater below. She shook her head in denial. "Not speaking to me?" he teased. Again, she shook her head. The thought hadn't really occurred to her until he suggested it, but she let him think what he wished. To her surprise, the experience of being aboard the yacht was proving to be fun, and she refused to let Jonathan spoil it for her. If she had to ignore him to preserve her sanity, so be it. She soon saw, however, that ignoring him would be very difficult.

"That's Isle au Haut to port," he pointed to the island approaching on the left. Cynthia shaded her eyes with her hand as she looked toward the wooded mass rising high out of the sea. Continuing, he explained, "It was named by Champlain, as were many of these islands, in the early 1600s. High Island—very appropriate." Cynthia agreed, admiring up close the beauty that had only been hinted at in the distance from Three Pines.

Jonathan caught her eye momentarily before he, too, looked back at Isle au Haut. "The island was originally owned by a group of men who formed the Isle au Haut Company. They allowed neither women, children, nor dogs on the island. Wise move," he chuckled, parrying the look of annoyance she cast his way.

They tacked back and forth around the island, with Jonathan intermittently naming other islands in view—how did he remember, she wondered. There were so many—Flake Island, Kimball Island, York and Great Spoon, Merchant, Spruce, and Devil's Island—the list went on and on. Some were heavily wooded, others pure field, some straight granite.

Following her thoughts, he went on. "Large parts of New York, Boston and other cities on the East Coast have been built of granite from these islands. There are great quarries on many of them—totally abandoned now. It's sad, in a way," he rambled on, unconcerned by her silence, "almost like the stumps of wood left in a downed forest."

The hint of sadness in his words caught Cynthia's attention, as she turned her gaze to study his features. His profile was as breathtaking in its own right as the islands' which broke the horizon. Strength was in the set of his chin, fineness in the uneven slope of his nose, rakishness in the lock of hair that blew across his forehead. Her heart skipped a beat as he returned her gaze, the blueness of his eyes made all the more vivid in comparison with the cold gray of the water. His smile was too much for her, its warmth melting away any remaining anger she may have felt toward him. Quickly, distrustful of her own responses, she pointed to another island that had just emerged over the bow.

"What island is that?"

"They call it Swan's Island, named after Colonel James Swan. He was a self-made millionaire who bought the island with money from land speculation down South. He found himself in France during the French Revolution, where he worked to help his many friends, including one Marie Antoinette. Swan managed to get much of their

57

property out of France and to the States, but never made it himself. I think you know the rest of the story!" He grinned, with a hacking motion of his hand against his neck.

"You're a walking encyclopedia, aren't you," she quipped, thoroughly enjoying his informative monologue.

He shrugged his shoulders innocently. "When you've spent as many summers as I have in the neighborhood, you pick up a few gems. I only wish I could pick up a few of the gems that were on that boat from France. They say the originals are around here somewhere . . . ," he added with a mischievous grin.

His attention returned to the horizon. "Do you see that other island, the smaller one just north of Swan's? It is Outer Long Island. No more than fifty years ago its harbor had quite a reputation as a rendezvous for pirates and other disreputables. Seems there were many a wild night ashore," he chuckled.

They proceeded west into Frenchman's Bay, where Jonathan lowered the sails and propelled the boat by motor around its perimeter. "These are known as the Porcupines," he explained, pointing to the cluster of islands at the innermost part of the bay. Cynthia guessed correctly that the name derived from the spruce and balsam that shot up, quill-like, over the landscape. "There's Long Porcupine, Sheep Porcupine, Burnt Porcupine, even Bald Porcupine over there—see, the one whose quills have mostly disappeared?" he laughed, and she spontaneously joined him, the intimacy of the cabin in which they now stood, spacious as it was though in sharp contrast to the expanse of open deck they had left, beginning to affect her senses.

All thought of resisting his company, either through noncommunication or through belligerency, had vanished. She found herself increasingly drawn to him, both in sight and sound. She'd better create a diversion, she realized, or she would be tempted to succumb to his charm.

Mercifully, Jonathan's attention was caught by the harbor which lay ahead of them. "Bar Harbor. It was supposedly quite a place at the start of the century—huge estates and Victorian cottages overlooking Frenchman's Bay. Over the years its glitter faded, though, and the great fire of nineteen forty-seven destroyed what did remain. Today it is primarily a tourist center. However, because it is still a little early for the worst of the crowds, we'll see if we can find a mooring to tie up to, and then row ashore for lunch. Hungry?" he asked.

"You bet!" she exclaimed, her enthusiasm embarrassing her momentarily, unexpected as it was.

He grinned, agreeing, "So am I!," but the look he gave her suggested hunger of a different type, and Cynthia colored, feeling the return of her irritation—at him for his intimation and at herself for her sensitivity to it.

Skillfully, he guided the boat into the harbor and alongside a mooring, cut the motor, and let Cynthia take over at the wheel while he tied up securely. Naturally, he handled the rowboat like an expert, as he had the yacht. Quite the jack-of-all-trades, she noted, begrudgingly; too bad he had to botch up his romantic liaisons!

Once ashore, he guided her to a small restaurant, away from the hub of the harbor, but with a beautiful view of the bay nevertheless. He appeared to know the owners well, being greeted warmly by the husband and wife team and introducing them to Cynthia as old friends. There were no menus offered; Jonathan ordered for them both, a gesture whose intimacy excited Cynthia almost as much as their proximity to one another across the small table. And his choice was just what she might have ordered herself: a lobster salad, with huge chunks of the sweet and succulent meat nesting on a bed of romaine lettuce and garnished with a variety of condiments, fresh-from-the-oven biscuits with a tub of homemade butter, and a large bottle of Chablis.

To her amazement, the conversation was as amiable as the food was mouth-watering. It was as though by silent and mutual consent they had buried the hatchet, for the day at least. He asked her questions about her uncle, and she freely explained how her parents had died and her uncle had been so good to her. He asked about her schooling, showing genuine interest—too much so, she asked herself—in the fact that her dissertation was on drug use and abuse, but she quickly forgot her suspicion in the excitement of answering his questions about her paper.

"Your study is remarkable, Cynthia," he acknowledged respectfully. "It's just too bad there have to be any studies on the subject." He grew suddenly serious. "The flow of marijuana into this country, for one thing, is at flood proportions. We just can't seem to stop it. The East Coast alone offers countless points of entry for smugglers." He stared at his wine glass, now empty, his suppressed anger, and indeed his very knowledge of the subject, surprising her.

She filled in for him, anxious to keep him talking so that she could find the source of both the anger and the interest. "Santa Marta Gold, it's called. The best that Colombia has to offer!" she remarked sarcastically.

He looked up at her, some inner motive generating an intensity of feeling that burst forth through his expression. "It's brought up in large freighters, called 'mother ships,' which then transfer the goods to smaller cruisers and souped-up speedboats from local ports." He gestured with his hand toward the bay which they now overlooked, suggesting that even its seeming purity could be deceiving.

Cynthia was genuinely curious, with Jonathan so informed on the subject. "I don't understand why the Coast Guard isn't able to do more to apprehend both—the mother ships and the smaller transports."

"It's a touchy issue," he smiled sadly. "The Coast Guard has no authority as long as the freighters stay outside the

60

twelve-mile limit, which they usually do. And even with the smaller boats that bring the stuff ashore . . . well, there's so much corruption among officials involved that apprehension is at a minimum. Added on top of that, the rising cost of fuel has greatly curtailed the regular pot patrols, and there were too few of them to begin with!" Cynthia saw his jaw tighten in frustration and sensed, instinctively, that his was not just a passing interest in the subject.

"You seem deeply involved," she commented. His head jerked up, and she saw the look of dismay on his face. Then he lowered his gaze once again.

"I once knew a girl . . . a real beauty . . ." He glanced at her hesitantly, unsure as to how she would take hearing about his past relationships. Her expression was completely passive, as she tenaciously willed it to be. He went on. "She used the stuff regularly . . . until the day she bought a bad bag. It may have been the alcohol, too. She was in a coma when I saw her in the hospital . . . and died a week later. Her family was devastated," he concluded. Cynthia's eyes never left his face. She wasn't sure how to respond, knowing too well the familiar story, yet sensing that his involvement with the issue went further than this one friend. All she knew was that the conversation had taken a heavier turn than she wanted on this particular day. She made a move to remedy the situation.

"Tell me about yourself. You handle boats well. Have you always summered with them?"

He smiled, though she wondered whether it was in acknowledgment of her compliment or in cognizance of her change of subject. If it was a case of the latter, he didn't resist. "I grew up on them. My folks owned one of those mansions that used to be here," he jerked his head sideways toward the greenery of Bar Harbor. "It burned down with the rest and we never rebuilt, but I still managed to spend most of my summers at one place or another along the coast."

"How long have you owned the island?"

"It will be seven years this summer. What do you think of it?" He was testing her responses, but she spoke with full honesty.

"It's magnificent! I've never spent any time on an island before. It could become addictive . . ." She caught her breath at her unfortunate choice of words, then chose to ignore her slip. "Is your cottage similar to mine?"

He nodded. "By and large. It is a little bigger, has an extra room, and it has a fireplace at its center."

"Ah ha!" she grinned. "I thought I smelled the luscious aroma of burning wood! Where do you go on that lobster boat every day?" She hadn't thought twice about her forwardness, the atmosphere had been so open and friendly, but there was a tense moment as he looked sharply at her.

"So you watch my comings and goings, do you?" he taunted, an overtone in his voice that she didn't understand.

Cynthia was immediately on the defensive. "It's my job to be a watchdog, isn't it? And, anyway, when your walls are made of glass, you don't miss much of what goes on."

"So I can imagine. Do you also watch me swimming in the nude every morning?" he drawled suggestively.

Her denial was immediate. "You don't swim in the nude! I've seen you coming out of the water wearing a— oh, you're impossible!" she exclaimed in embarrassment, realizing that she had fallen into his trap, and she looked out toward the harbor as her face reddened under his hearty burst of laughter.

When he had sufficiently composed himself, he leaned toward her intimately, his breath warm against her ear, sending reluctant currents of excitement through her. "I'm glad to see you're doing your job," he murmured seductively. "Now, shall we go?"

She rose quickly, grateful to break the spell that his nearness cast each and every time over her. What was the matter with her, she asked herself for the hundredth time. Why was she so weak in his presence? She was usually in total control; why the lapse now? What were these feelings that flooded her senses at the sight and sound of him? And, above all, how could she so callously forget the voluptuous blonde in the red chiffon dress? She pondered these questions as she made her escape to the safety of the street, where Jonathan shortly joined her.

They returned to the yacht and set sail once again, this time heading south by the Cranberry Isles and around Mount Desert Island. Once again, Jonathan was the tour guide. "Champlain was responsible for the naming of this one, too. 'L'isle des Monts Desert,' he called it—island of the barren mountains. The panorama of the hills is spectacular, don't you think? That's Cadillac Mountain over there; maybe you'd like to climb it one day."

"I might just do that," she agreed enthusiastically, having successfully regained her composure following its momentary loss at lunch. They sailed through Blue Hill Bay and then up into Eggemoggin Reach, with Jonathan relating this or that anecdote about the places they passed.

It was late in the afternoon when they passed North Haven and rounded Vinalhaven, heading north once more to pass Isle au Haut on the way to Three Pines. The wind had picked up and Cynthia was grateful that Jonathan had taken her heavy sweater from its hanger back at the cottage. Despite the long day, she felt exhilarated by it, inwardly reluctant to see the peak of Three Pines emerge in the fast fading daylight.

But Jonathan was no more eager than she to dock just yet. Had he sensed her reluctance to see the day end, she wondered, hoping desperately that she had not been quite that transparent. Having lowered the sails, he motored the yacht to the opposite side of the island, overlooking the mainland, where he anchored at a safe distance from the rocky promontory that dominated this westerly face and looked all the more ominous for the cold blue light of dusk.

"What are we doing now?" Cynthia demanded, suddenly distrustful of his intentions.

His calm tone made hers seem almost panicked by comparison. "The chef will prepare dinner while the professor looks at the sights," he quipped, having joined her at the stern of the craft. Placing one arm on her shoulder, he pointed with the other. "The lights are just coming on. Look . . . there's Stonington . . ." It was a beautiful sight, looking back over the water at the distant mainland, the signs of civilization studding the landscape intermittently. Cynthia tried to concentrate on them, to the exclusion of Jonathan's touch, which, searing through the layers of fabric, fought hard for her undivided attention. For what seemed an eternity, she battled her impulses, those of the mind versus those of the body; then suddenly the battle ended as Jonathan disappeared into the cabin, and she was left with the ghost of his touch, heavy in memory on her shoulder, making her mind's victory a shallow one.

Although she felt guilty letting him prepare dinner without an offer of help, she feared there would be much more to feel guilty about should she descend into the galley. It was a small area, she remembered from her exploration earlier in the day, and she feared for her self-control in such close proximity to him. Rather, she would cool off for a bit and try to regain some of the strength she hoped she had.

All too soon, the cry came up. "Dinner's ready!" Jonathan emerged to guide her to the dinette, a compactly outfitted lounge area behind the cockpit. He had prepared a simple dinner, cooked to perfection—steak and broccoli, with a hollandaise sauce which she envied. The wine he chose, a hearty burgundy, suited the menu perfectly, though she resolved to drink as little as possible; she would need every last bit of self-control to counter the intimacy of the meal.

The conversation was as stimulating as it had been earlier in the day. Cynthia felt herself becoming more and more enthralled by this tall, godlike figure of a man. Was he always this charming, she wondered? Or had he poured it on just for her benefit, an objective clear in his mind? She wouldn't let herself be snared thus, like a sheep being led to the slaughter.

Striking out in self-defense, she cornered him. "Do you always wine and dine your women this way?" Her eyes looked into his, mildly accusing.

He grinned mischievously. "Do you consider yourself one of 'my women,' as you so delicately put it?"

"Certainly not!" she blurted back, furious that her tactic had backfired so easily. A flush rose to her cheeks as her anger grew, not caused by any happening on this day—despite its ominous start, it had been a glorious day, in her private estimation—but in remembrance of last Saturday night when she had felt so utterly hurt and humiliated.

She lowered her voice, hoping he wouldn't notice its slight tremor. "Doesn't it get a little repetitious? I mean, did you serve your blond-haired darling the same menu?" she sneered, even as she chided herself for the low blow.

Jonathan stared at her across the table, his expression somber. Cynthia noticed for the first time the furrows on his forehead as his eyebrows drew together in a suggestion of—was it hurt? So her arrow had hit its target, she mused, although without any sense of victory. To the contrary, her impulse was to jump up, throw her arms around his neck in apology, and kiss away the worry lines that made him look every bit his 37 years.

Instead, she merely lowered her eyes and whispered, "I'm sorry. That was unnecessary. I'm not usually that vicious. I don't know what's gotten into me . . ." Her voice trailed off as she stood up and walked to the stairs leading to the deck, where she was greeted by a cool draft of salt air.

The steady sound of the ocean prevented her from hearing soft footsteps behind her. She jumped as strong hands slipped around her waist and a deep voice murmured huskily in her ear, "Don't you?"

She had lingered a little too long, savoring the touch of his long body against hers. When she turned toward him to deny his inference, his mouth seized her parted lips, devouring them in the torrent of passion which had been building all day. There was no teasing, no gentle invitation, as there had been before. Rather, his possession was a fait accompli, a command that Cynthia had no choice but to obey. Her pulse raced madly, her mind a whirling mass of confusion when he withdrew his lips from their bruising onslaught. His face was close to hers, bare inches away. She looked into his eyes, blazing with something that could have been anger as easily as passion. She inhaled the musky male smell of him, an aphrodisiac in itself.

Slowly and of their own volition, her arms crept to his neck in subtle invitation. What was she doing, her mind screamed! Her senses told her a different story. The gentle pressure of her hands in the warm hair at the nape of his neck was all he needed to bridge these few inches and seize her lips again. There was gentleness now, of a firm and masculine type, as he coaxed her into reciprocation. To her dismay, she found herself doing just that, returning his kisses with an abandon that frightened her.

Something was happening to her senses, she panicked, even as she tightened her neck-hold and parted her lips for his deeper embrace. She felt herself falling, falling, into some starry abyss which had no bottom. But Jonathan's hands were around her, stroking her shoulders and back, pressing her toward him until she arched her body in

66

yearning, delighting in the intimate fit of his every contour against her own.

Drugged by the smoldering passion, she made no protest as he swung her off her feet and into his arms, carrying her as though she weighed no more than a child, then laying her with a most adult tenderness on the wide sofa that stretched the length of the cabin. He lowered himself beside her, clasped his hands in hers, and drew them over her head. Pinning her thus, his lips commenced a breathtaking exploration of her eyes, nose, cheeks, and chin, searing a path down her throat to the open vee of her blouse. Cynthia felt the pleasure burst within her, moaning in frustration at being unable to return his caress.

Sensing her need, he released her hands to their impassioned travels over his sinewy shoulders and through his vitally thick hair. In so doing, he had also freed his own hands to probe further Cynthia's feminine resources. In an instant, he had unbuttoned her blouse and pushed it aside, his hand cupping her firming breast, stroking, caressing as his mouth conveyed his rising ardor to hers.

Cynthia felt moved past all reason. These sensations that held her captive were new and beautiful beyond description. They were the most basic and primitive of instincts, the most natural of her very being. She slipped her hands under his shirt, reveling in the feel of his warm chest, firm yet pliant and terribly exciting. A sigh of pure ecstasy escaped her lips as his sought the pink buds of her breasts, laid open to him above the bra that he had so deftly eased aside.

The ache in her loins had become unbearable, the flame of passion all-consuming. The awareness of his own arousal as he moved atop her thrilled her all the more, heightening her desire for his total possession to an explosive level.

It was only when she opened her eyes and momentarily caught the reflection of the bobbing red light of another

67

yacht passing in the night that she remembered a blur of red chiffon from another night. It was that moment of sanity which saved her from total commitment; without it she would have been lost.

With all her strength, she pushed Jonathan away from her, an impossible feat had he not simultaneously begun to ease off. He gave her just enough room to swing her legs onto the floor and sit up, though his arms still straddled her hips, his body still close to hers.

She put a hand to her forehead as she realized how close she had come to giving Jonathan that which she had given to no other man; the thought set off an uncontrollable trembling throughout her body.

"Don't be afraid, Cynthia," he murmured, kissing her neck tenderly as he spoke. She pulled her head away.

"You don't understand," she cried miserably, shaking her head as though to dislodge the image of the beautiful blonde and thus deny her existence. But she did exist; there was no escaping that fact!

"I do understand that we are attracted to one another. I saw how you responded. I know how I responded. Can you deny it?" She shook her head unhappily. He continued, his voice deep with a feeling she hadn't expected and which upset her all the more. "I won't hurt you . . ." He put his arms around her to still her trembling.

Her eyes pierced his then, the fight in her brown orbs matching the glitter of his blues. "There are many ways of hurting someone."

He stiffened suddenly and moved away from her, although not without a look of disappointment, nay, disgust. So that was all he wanted—an outlet for his physical urges. And she had been foolish enough to think that he enjoyed her company as much as she had his! How naive can you be, Cynthia, she scolded herself, hastily buttoning the buttons which his experienced fingers had released in the heat of passion.

Sitting there, staring at his dark head and broad back as he gazed out the porthole, Cynthia realized that, regardless of his crude intentions, something had held him back, just as it had restrained her—the same something which had come between them that Saturday night had done so again. What was the power of this obstacle? Again, a sense of mystery engulfed her. There were too many questions that he avoided answering. What was the great puzzle of which this magnificently strong, devastatingly handsome man, who touched off a myriad of unexplored sensations within her, was the central piece?

The nameless blonde, the daily trips on a lobster boat, her own very presence on the island . . . there was neither reason nor rhyme. Yet something, newly awakened, now tucked away deep within Cynthia, began its mournful song.

CHAPTER FOUR

Cynthia reached a momentous decision at dawn the next morning, culminating a long and sleepless night. Jonathan had returned her to the cottage the evening before, purity—though little else—intact. During the subsequent hours of internal struggle, she ran the gamut of "why did he"s, "how could he"s, "how can I"s, "why should I"s, and "what if"s?

Two things emerged from this personal battle. First, she concluded that she was fast on her way to falling in love with Jonathan Roaman. Even her limited knowledge of him told her that he possessed all of the qualities she sought in a man, friend, husband, and lover. He was strong, both physically and emotionally; he was intelligent; he was interesting and interested; he was fun to be with; and he was very, very sexually appealing. The proof of the latter shook Cynthia to the core as the memory of his embrace flooded over her, intoxicating her senses anew.

But other emotions accompanied this exhilaration—shame, embarrassment, and a sense of betrayal. She had responded to him willingly and openly, knowing all the while that he was involved with another.

As she saw it, in the wee hours of the morning, there were two roads open to her. On the one, she could avoid Jonathan as much as possible, even leave the island if pressure became unbearable. But this was not Cynthia's way; she was a challenger, not a coward. Thus, she set herself on the other road, and in this her momentous decision was made.

She would stay where she was and doggedly try to piece together the bits of the puzzle which evaded her. If she failed, she would always have her work and her life back in Philadelphia to comfort her. If she succeeded, she would have something potentially longer lasting and infinitely more satisfying. It was this latter course that she knew she would have to follow, painful as it might prove to be. Unfortunately, the pain began all too soon.

Cynthia did not see Jonathan on Friday, although Saturday morning he knocked on the door to invite her to join him for a swim.

"Change and meet me on the beach in ten minutes!" he ordered in the face of her slight hesitation, and then he was off, leaving her to gaze admiringly at his deeply tanned back. Attractive as he had looked in his swimming gear from her distant window perch each morning, his physique was that much more compelling close up, as he had been just now. She wondered if she dared tempt fate by meeting him on the beach, then realized that she would be tempting fate all the more by not showing up. She had already seen his reaction to that kind of behavior!

Slipping into her swimsuit and grabbing a towel, she was met by a look of mock astonishment when she arrived on the beach moments later.

"I was getting ready to fetch you," he teased.

"Oh, no," she retorted. "I'm not *that* stupid!"

"Hey, you're getting the beginnings of a nice tan. You look much healthier," he drawled, eying the pink-beige

71

coloring surrounding her none-too generous bikini and sending an even healthier color to her cheeks.

She poked at the warm sand with her toes, avoiding his penetrating gaze. "I try to swim every day. You know, stretch the muscles and all . . ."

"Don't let me stop you," he smirked, remaining where he was on the sand.

Obediently, and grateful for the suggested escape, Cynthia dropped her towel to plunge into the waves, appreciating the cool relief from more than one kind of heat. Within moments, Jonathan had joined her, comfortably adapting his swimming pace to hers.

As she reflected afterward, it was a lovely interlude. He was a gentleman in every sense of the word; she enjoyed both the swim and the sunbath following, finding pleasure in Jonathan's company, though barely a word was exchanged. After about an hour, Cynthia felt she had had as much sun as was good for her at a stretch, her skin still relatively pale and sensitive in comparison with Jonathan's hearty tan.

"If you need anything in town, let me know. I'll be going in later," he stated nonchalantly as she was about to leave.

"As a matter of fact, I could use a few things. Maybe I'll go in with you," she suggested impulsively.

Immediately she realized her mistake. His tone cooled and he became suddenly angry. "That wouldn't be a very good idea. I won't be coming back directly, although I can store anything perishable in the icebox aboard until I do get here. Just make a list," he commanded, dismissing her abruptly.

As Cynthia scrambled up the path, smarting from his verbal blow, she began to understand. A pattern emerged: the Saturday afternoon trip to Stonington, the return with supplies and . . . what else? She would wait and see if her suspicions were correct.

It was too dark to see much of anything when the yacht docked that evening. Knowing that she was in a goldfish bowl in her glass-enclosed, lighted cabin, she stayed away from the panels deliberately. Jonathan dutifully delivered to her the things she had asked for, then quickly bade her good night before being swallowed up by the darkness. His dinner attire had not escaped Cynthia's attention. As he had been last Saturday night, he was more formally dressed than during the week, having dined in style, she concluded acidly.

Sure enough, the light of day gave proof to Cynthia's hypothesis. By mid-morning, Jonathan escorted his blonde-haired friend back to the yacht and they departed, under sail, for the mainland. Given her decision to uncover the great mystery, Cynthia resolved to ask him about this competition, but she would have to be careful to choose the right time and place for such an interrogation. In the meantime, the pain was devastating.

Cynthia delved head-on into her dissertation, attacking a particularly challenging analysis in hopes of taking her mind from the inevitable hurt. It worked . . . barely. She was fine as long as she kept herself buried under figures, but the mystery lurked at every break, just waiting to ensnare her again. She pushed herself mercilessly for the rest of the day, finally falling into bed late at night, unaware of whether or not Jonathan had returned.

Saturday

Dear Uncle William,

Greetings from Down East! It's been raining all day today, so I'm taking my break time to write you when I'd normally be swimming (no offense intended). You'd be amazed at how much I've accomplished in the two weeks (is that all?) since I arrived. It's the perfect location for serious study; I highly recommend it! I try to work all day, with an hour or two off at noontime to relax, swim, and sunbathe. Not the bad life at all, and I will have some tan to camouflage the circles under my eyes!

Seriously, I am also getting plenty of rest. The brisk night air is conducive to deep sleep, as I'm sure my volume of work is also! Never fear—it seems that Jonathan Roaman is of the same mind as you are (are you two by chance in cahoots with one another?). He is determined to make me do something other than work—and when he gets determined, it is very difficult to buck him!

I must confess that despite my preconceptions, he is a nice person . . . you'd like him! I don't see him that often, though. Would you believe that he goes out lobstering every day? When I finally got up the courage to ask him where he disappeared to, I was amazed. He is working for the summer (taking time off from his big business, which he claims runs itself with only an occasional checking up by him) with a local fellow named Dick Young. I met him once; he is a laconic sort, as so many of them are supposed to be, with a dark look about him, but, according to Jonathan, a skilled lobsterman. I've been invited to go lobstering with them one day next week, and I may just accept!

Several evenings ago, Jonathan dragged me bodily away from my typewriter and down to the beach to sample the day's catch. I'm still not sure which was more exquisite—the lobster or the sunset! So you can rest assured that there are diversions here. No, no, Uncle William, don't rest assured *that* much . . . if I read your calculating mind from this distance. Jonathan has a steady girl who spends every Saturday night here, so ours is a simple friendship. Period.

I'm playing the perfect watchdog, though there's

not really much to that job. However, I do spy my boss down on the landing now, and if I don't get this letter to him it will miss the evening mail.

> Your affectionate niece,
> Cynthia

In retrospect, Cynthia was pleased with herself at having fitted one more piece into the puzzle. Jonathan had not been about to offer any information on his own and it had been only after some gentle prodding, and many attempted evasions on his part, that she had learned of the lobstering.

"But why do you work during your own vacation?" she had asked him at the time.

"Very simple—I love it!" he had answered succinctly, taking after the lobstermen, themselves, in this regard.

"It must be tiring to go out every day . . ."

"Not tiring. Invigorating. Exhilarating. Not tiring," he had firmly corrected her, his blue eyes sparkling blindingly down on her.

It was one further insight into a man who, she was quickly discovering, was as multifaceted as he was multimillioned. Cynthia felt respect growing along with the other emotions that swept her, although she was cautious to reveal only the bare essentials to her uncle.

It was early Wednesday morning, as she stole a glance at him swimming, that he grinned and waved directly at her. She had hoped that her observances went unnoticed; what an arrogant man he was to assume—correctly, much to her mortification—that she would be watching him! Moments later, he appeared at the door, hair and skin glistening from the salt water, looking breathtakingly masculine in his snug-fitting swim suit.

75

"Put on something heavy and meet me at the pier. You're coming lobstering today," he declared, his eyes defying her to object.

Cynthia's heart pounded with excitement, but pride forced her to resist. "I can't go today." She gestured at the table behind her littered with piles of papers. "I've just begun all this—"

"You can work on it tomorrow," he answered gruffly. "It will be a fine day today for lobstering, cloudy enough so you won't get burned. Dick will be here soon, so be quick about it!" He was off, leaving her openmouthed in protest.

It *was* a perfect day for lobstering. Lightly overcast, the sun was no threat to her skin. Neither were the waves to her stomach, as the boat gently rode the surface, bobbing occasionally between the swells. Jonathan kept up a steady monologue on the technique of lobstering, and although Cynthia caught Dick eying her warily once or twice, the latter was either too preoccupied with his work to make additions or corrections, or simply disinterested.

"How do you know which traps are yours?" she queried, as they motored to an area of ocean where several other boats were simultaneously pulling traps.

Jonathan smiled understandingly, his eye following hers to the army of buoys jousting on the surface. "Each buoy is painted with the colors of a particular lobsterman. Kind of like racing colors. Needless to say, each man respects the other's buoys."

"What about tourists? Can't they pull the traps as easily?"

"It's not usually a problem," he explained. "Most people don't have the equipment or the stamina to get the traps up. And many of them would want neither themselves nor their boats to get dirty!" He laughed, looking around him at the telltale signs of yesterday's work.

Cynthia immediately understood, as she watched the

two men retrieve a green and white buoy, attach its line to the sturdy winch on deck, and then run it off the engine's motor to pull the string of traps, one by one, to the surface.

Jonathan elaborated. "Years ago, this was done by hand, a much slower project. Virtually all of these boats are equipped with motor-driven winches today."

"How many traps do you have, Dick?" She attempted to get a response from the silent one.

"Near three hundred," he answered laconically, and Cynthia knew she had lost him again for a while.

Jonathan must have been amused at her expression of dismay at Dick's clipped manner. "Lobstermen are a breed of independent men . . . conversation is superfluous for them. Isn't that so, Dick?" he smiled, smoothing over the rough edge that had appeared.

Again, the response was short and to the point. "A-yah."

Cynthia barely stifled the burst of laughter that threatened to escape at his stereotypical reply. Fortunately she succeeded enough to avoid his misinterpretation of her most innocent reaction. Why did she get the uncomfortable feeling that Dick would rather not have her aboard?

The first of the traps had been emptied into an underneath bin, but not before Dick and Jonathan had secured thick rubber bands around the claws of the lobsters.

"What are the wooden pegs I remember seeing on some of them?" she asked, puzzled by the elastic bands.

"Those are still used by some lobstermen to hold the claws shut, but the trend is toward using these rubber-bands instead. This way there is no chance of injuring any of the meat that is edible," Jonathan explained patiently, as he held out one lobster which was snapping fiercely.

Cynthia backed off a few steps, muttering, "It's a good thing you're wearing heavy gloves. Just remember that I'm not!"

Jonathan laughed aloud, a devilish twinkle in his eye. "I didn't think you were afraid of anything! Sure, this lobster could cut one of the smaller ones in half, that's why we bind his claws, but you, Cynthia, are made of harder fabric, as I recall . . ." His words trailed off, their implication clear; Cynthia shot him a scornful look and turned away. Why did he deride her, in front of Dick, no less? Just because she had refused to capitulate to his physical demands? Well, he could just continue to satisfy himself with his one-night-a-week date, for all she cared!

But she did care, very much. It was this caring that she camouflaged as she forced herself to reply coldly. "That's right. I'm a firm believer in the survival of the fittest, and I'll be damned if I'll be broken in two by some claw!"

Cynthia couldn't believe what she heard next. "Dick, you'll have to excuse us. This is an ongoing argument. As for you, Cynthia, if you're referring to Suzanne, I can guess that she has never had to resort to clawing. Stroking, yes. Caressing, yes. But never clawing. It's not her way, which is why I look forward to seeing her every weekend." Again, Cynthia turned away from Jonathan, this time to prevent him from seeing the tears that had materialized in the wake of his cutting remark. Why did he make a point of humiliating her? Was he that cruel?

She made no effort to return her attention to the men's work. The human silence seemed endless, broken only by the sounds of traps being rebaited and dropped back into the ocean, and, of course, the steady sound of the ocean. It was the latter that calmed Cynthia and enabled her to regain her composure.

Jonathan said nothing until Dick had entered the cabin and started the engine to move to a different group of traps, when he would be out of earshot.

He approached her and laid a hand on her shoulder, for an instant, to attract her attention. "I'm sorry, Cynthia. The last thing I want to do is hurt you."

78

Now anger clouded her eyes. "That's a likely story. You love humiliating me . . . don't deny it. But in front of him," she cocked her head in the direction of the cabin, "Was that necessary?" She pleaded for an explanation, unable to find one herself.

He looked tensely down at the cold water. "Yes, it was." Then he turned to her, an unfathomable expression in his eyes. "One day I'll be able to explain to you. I can't just now." It was impossible for Cynthia to understand his motive, yet she imagined she saw a depth of feeling entering his gaze. "You have to trust me. Please?" he urged softly.

The fact that he had *asked* her rather than *told* her communicated something extra to Cynthia. Then, very gently, he touched the back of his hand to her cheek, and she forgave him everything. At that instant, the engine quieted and Jonathan turned to prepare the winch for the next stringer.

Cynthia couldn't have remained angry with him had she tried. Strangely, she did trust him, although she didn't know why. She knew that he felt something for her—unless he was a supreme actor. There was so much that still puzzled her. One thing she knew: Time was her strongest ally.

Miraculously, they were both able to bounce back and salvage the day from potential ruin. It appeared to Cynthia that Dick saw it as a misadventure anyway, scowling at her now and then, particularly as she posed the questions that continually popped into her curious mind.

"Hey, what are you doing?" she yelled, as he tossed back into the ocean several of the lobsters from the latest bunch of traps.

"Too small," was his terse reply as he cast an annoyed glance her way before continuing his work.

It was Jonathan who explained. "There are legal limits, size-wise, to what we can keep. The lobsters can't be over four pounds or under one. Also, we have to throw back any females with eggs. The lobster population is depleted enough."

A little later, when the traps were being rebaited, she asked, waving a hand back and forth before her nose, "Pfew! What do you use for bait? That's quite a smell!"

"Cod, mackerel, other fish, and shellfish," Jonathan replied, circumventing Dick's silence. "Aged in bait sheds . . . the stronger the smell, the better. You see, lobsters are the scavengers of the sea. These traps lie on the ocean floor where the lobsters crawl around eating practically everything in sight. It's a miracle people still want to eat them, considering what makes their meat so succulent." He chuckled, and Cynthia joined him.

"Can't they cut their way out of the traps once they've eaten the bait?"

"Nope," Dick interjected somberly, following the conversation but opting out of it for the most part, other than his occasional one-worder.

Jonathan smiled at his curtness, kidding him, "They don't say much, do they!"

"Nope," the lobsterman repeated, the barest suggestion of a smile on his lips as he caught the ambiguity in Jonathan's words.

"Actually," Jonathan went on, for Cynthia's benefit, "these same style traps have been used since the mid-sixteen hundreds. Classic, aren't they?" he grinned, scrutinizing one as he reloaded it with bait and threw it over the side of the boat.

"I could really use one as a scarf bin," Cynthia pondered aloud, "if I could find one that doesn't smell quite so badly," she giggled at the thought.

And so the day progressed, with no further antagonism between Jonathan and Cynthia and only minor grating when it came to Dick. From her viewpoint as a spectator, Cynthia found the whole operation intriguing. She would have helped out, in fact, had not Jonathan refused her offer, although she suspected that he was deferring to Dick's sentiments.

It was late in the afternoon when they were dropped back at the dock.

"Where does he go from here?" Cynthia asked Jonathan, as they watched the lobster boat pull away from the pier and head toward the southern tip of the island.

"He'll turn the catch in to the pound at Stonington on his way home. The lobsters will be stored in the harbor and trucked out from there."

"He's an odd character," she remarked, as the boat disappeared from sight.

Jonathan turned to look at her, as ruggedly handsome as ever after the hard day's work. The orange cast of the declining sun outlined his features, giving then added drama. He didn't say a word, yet the message sent by his shimmering blue eyes was hard to miss.

Cynthia thought quickly. "I believe I owe you a dinner," she began. "You earned your keep today! Does he pay you . . . or the other way around?"

"Neither. And I thought you'd never offer! I am famished! Now it's your turn to work. Do you still have those lamb chops?" He had taken firm command, yet Cynthia could not resist the opportunity to challenge him.

"Just a minute. When you cook, *you* decide the menu. When I cook, it's my choice. Be at my place in half an hour," she ordered, pleased at having given him a dose of his own medicine.

"And if I'm not?" he baited her.

She balked at carrying the analogy that far. "Then it will be your loss," she retorted, and, with a tilt of her chin, she proceeded up the pier toward the shadowy hillside.

Sure enough, thirty minutes later Jonathan showed up, freshly showered and clothed, and smelling dangerously of damp masculinity and a touch of aftershave. Cynthia was grateful she had changed into her white slacks and lavender pullover, a sight dressier than the jeans she had worn all day, and much more compatible with Jonathan's gray slacks and Irish knit sweater. As warm as the days could become, the nights on the island were downright chilly, she had quickly discovered!

"A gift for the hostess," Jonathan exclaimed, gallantly producing a bottle of red wine.

"Perfect! Red wine—it will go with the . . . "

"Lamb chops," he supplied smugly.

"That's unfair," she protested mildly. "It's no wonder you have an inventory of my supplies since you do the marketing. If you'd let me go with you some Saturday, I could surprise you," she taunted, awaiting the inevitable rise from him.

He proceeded to the kitchen drawer for a corkscrew and opened the wine without a comment. Cynthia waited; surely he would jump at the bait. Instead he turned, handed her a glass of wine, and then touched it with his own.

"To a nice day! You did enjoy yourself, didn't you?" Cynthia couldn't read his expression, but she tried desperately to erase the look of dismay on hers. All right; she'd play along with him for a bit.

"I did, thank you," she conceded, sipping her wine. "How did you connect with Dick in the first place?"

"I wanted to spend my summer lobstering, and he was willing to take a helper along. He's very professional," he reasoned.

"I don't know . . . he seems too serious, almost sullen to me. Are all lobstermen like that?" she asked doubtfully.

"Lobstermen are a rare breed. They are independent hard workers who prize their freedom. They make their own schedules, and see the direct results of their work each day. The only superior they work under is nature herself. She can be a harsh mistress, able to make or break in a season. The monetary rewards are very good, though, for the average lobsterman today. Dick must do very well for himself," he stated.

"I hope so, for his sake." Then she wondered aloud, "He didn't want me around today, did he?"

A troubled look flitted across Jonathan's features. "That is just his manner. I wouldn't worry about it." But she did feel uneasy, almost threatened, and barely comforted by Jonathan's own frown. It was a long moment before she moved to the broiler.

"The chops will be ready in a minute. Have a seat," she suggested as she deftly tossed the salad.

Perhaps it was the wine that gave her boldness; perhaps she had merely tired of wondering. But when the lamb had been demolished and the salad and rolls similarly done in, Cynthia broached the subject again.

"Who is Suzanne?" she ventured bluntly.

Jonathan slowly raised his eyes to hers, the blue crystals turned to ice in surprise at her forthrightness. She returned his gaze in a stubborn refusal to be stared down. His face gave no hint of his thoughts; only his eyes spoke, chilling her to the bone. His voice was nearly as cold when the words finally came.

"Her name is Suzanne DeCarlo. She is my secretary and a very good friend."

"Isn't that understating it?" she accused.

"Why do you say that?" he barked back.

"Well, she spends every Saturday night with you. Wouldn't you call that a little more than just friendship?"

His lips had thinned and he seemed to be controlling himself from an outburst he might regret. "You can draw whatever conclusion you like." He arose abruptly from the table and stalked to the window.

Reluctant to forfeit the present opportunity, she joined

him there, following his gaze to the traces of sunset that lingered on the far horizon.

Putting her hands in her pockets, she spoke softly. "I don't know what conclusion to draw. One day you come on to me; another you shack up with her."

He twirled around to face her and was about to shake her when he saw the look in her eyes. Quickly she turned away, but not soon enough to hide the vulnerability written on her face; her only hope was that he had not grasped its totality.

He replied in a low, clipped tone. "You don't know what you're talking about . . . and I resent your choice of words."

It suddenly occurred to Cynthia that maybe she didn't know what she was saying. She had, like a fool, implied that he had some special feeling for her when, in fact, the only special feelings he had were saved for Suzanne. The only feeling he had for her was lust! How could she have been so stupid? Men used women all the time; why couldn't she see that Jonathan was using her now?

"I guess not," she whispered in agreement, as she fled to the sink to begin cleaning up.

It must have been a full five minutes before she dared look over her shoulder. Jonathan had not moved, but remained, staring out at the now darkened water. She finished washing the broiler pan before she approached him.

"I think you'd better leave now," she suggested, quietly but firmly.

He eyed her deliberately, sending a shudder of desire through her. The one place she truly wanted to be was in his arms, yet it was the one place that frightened her most. For once there, she feared she might not have the strength to pull away. Even knowing that she meant nothing to Jonathan, her own feelings toward him were so strong that she was helpless to refuse him. Tears of frustration gathered behind her lids and she lowered her eyes to hide their betrayal.

Jonathan raised his hands to her arms, rubbing them from shoulder to elbow, as he murmured softly, "Stick with me, Cynthia. Don't give up." Very gently he pulled her against the warm wall of his chest until his heartbeat hammered in her ear. The slight tremor of his otherwise strong arms, as they encircled her, came as a surprise, the emotion it implied confusing her all the more. When he released her after a moment, he walked quietly to the door and left.

Cynthia sank down by the window in a stupor. She had no idea what to believe. If anything, her prodding had only deepened the mystery, rather than having the opposite and intended effect. She cried herself to sleep that night, as she had not done in many a year.

Cynthia kept very much to herself for the next few days, avoiding Jonathan at every opportunity. He, in turn, appeared to respect her wishes on that score. Although he spent his days lobstering, she plodded along with her dissertation, taking only an occasional break, pushing herself harder than ever. Her work was to be her only salvation, she feared.

By Friday afternoon, she was exhausted and, realizing that it might be her last chance to have the beach in total privacy until the beginning of the week, she made her way to its sandy stretch. Despite the brilliant sun, or perhaps in contrast to it, the water seemed particularly cold as she plunged into the waves. For a few minutes, she kept up the brisk pace, which the water temperature inspired. It was only when her muscles began to tire that she slowed and headed back to shore.

She was only about one hundred feet from her goal when something happened that was to be an omen of things to come. She had lapsed into a restful breaststroke when her leg suddenly knocked against something, sending

85

a sharp jab to her thigh. Instinctively, she quickened her stroke to escape whatever it was she had hit—or had hit her. Visions flashed through her mind, fueled by recent motion picture dramas, no doubt, of a severed limb, yet she still felt hers, both of them, hastening their flutter kick behind her. Propelled by panic, she moved along the surface, willing her body, as it were, away from the threat below. As her feet touched bottom, she scrambled frantically out of the water, and only when she had reached her towel and dry sand did she stop to look, first at her thigh, which showed no obvious sign of any injury, and then at the water, which was likewise devoid of anything extraordinary. She saw neither the horrifying fin of a shark, which, in her state of aroused imagination, she had half expected, nor the telltale jagged rock, which might have suggested that she had merely swam off course.

The experience was a quandary. Could she have been stung by some sea animal lurking close to shore? A jellyfish, perhaps? Yet she could find no sign on her thigh of any such sting. And she felt all right otherwise . . . or so she thought, until a sudden wave of dizziness overtook her and she sank down onto her stomach on the sand, oblivious to the entire happening.

Her next moment of consciousness came much, much later. "Cynthia! Cynthia! Can you hear me?" She struggled to raise her eyelids, but the weights that held them down were awesome. She tried to lift herself from the sand, but her skin felt taut, smarting painfully with each effort. Something cool and wet was on her forehead and her neck; only then did the world resume its proper tilt.

"You little fool!" growled a voice that she barely recognized as Jonathan's, and a hand reached to assist her as she sat up with a wince of pain.

"Acch . . . wh-what happened?" she stammered, holding her head as the horizon took a few last dips and dives.

"I'd like you to tell me that," he demanded angrily. "I've been trying to wake you up for five minutes!"

Cynthia was just beginning to assimilate what had indeed happened. "What are you doing here?" she asked, astonished that he was back on the island in the middle of the day.

"It's late. Dick just dropped me back and I saw you lying here. What kind of imbecile falls asleep on the beach like this? You've got one hell of a sunburn, or hadn't you anticipated that?" The fury in his eyes made Cynthia shrink back, but as she did so her back screamed again and she knew he was right.

"What t-time is it?" she whispered.

"Half past five. How long have you been here?" he demanded.

She looked down at the sand blindly, trying to draw facts out of the blur. "Since about one, I think . . . "

"How could you have slept for over four hours out here? Don't you get any sleep at night?" He was yelling by now, and her head had begun to ache terribly. She put both hands to her temples to ease their throbbing.

"I wasn't sleeping . . . something happened . . . I just got dizzy . . . I'm not sure what it was," she offered broken thoughts as they came to her. Whether it was her words or the tears in her eyes as she raised them to Jonathan's, he suddenly softened, a look of concern replacing that of anger on his face.

"What do you mean, Cynthia?" he asked quietly.

Patiently he listened as she retold the bare facts she could recall. Although it wasn't much of a story, he remained as serious, almost alarmed, as she finished.

"Let me see your leg," he ordered and, as she pointed to the right one, he examined it closely for any sign of a wound. "I don't see anything, and I have no idea what could have knocked you out for so long. Maybe you were just overtired," he accused, though mildly this time, as opposed to his earlier fury.

The combination of anger, fear, and bewilderment gave Cynthia the strength to contradict him forcefully. "I was not! I think I know myself pretty well by now. What happened to me this afternoon was *not* caused by exhaustion. I'm sure of that!" She made a valiant effort to stand up, finally succeeding only with Jonathan's help and a few painful exclamations.

She managed to get back to the cabin under her own power, though Jonathan stayed at her elbow as a precaution. Her headache had reached thunderous proportions by the time she stretched onto her stomach on the sofa and she gave no further thought to Jonathan as she lay in misery, desperately wishing she would pass out again and thus be relieved of her discomfort.

"Here, take these." Jonathan coaxed her into swallowing several aspirins. "They'll help the headache and the fever."

Weakly she looked at him. "Fever?"

"It's not only your back that is burning up," he explained, placing a cool hand to her forehead. "I'd make a guess that you have sunstroke as well. I've got the windows wide open, in case you hadn't noticed. Any cooler and I may freeze," he teased, but she was beyond the humor as she dropped her head limply onto a pillow.

Out of the confusion that now seized her fevered brain, she heard Jonathan's voice, calm and reassuring. "I'm going up the hill to get some lotion for your burn. Lie here and rest. Understand?" She nodded; mercifully, he hadn't tried to touch her inflamed skin and she wondered how she would survive the administering of a salve.

Very painfully, she was soon to discover. When Jonathan returned, he brought a large bottle of medication. "It will be easier for you if I use my hand to put this on," he explained as he proceeded to apply the lotion liberally over every bit of sunburn, from her shoulders to her back and hips, around her bikini, to her legs. In other circumstances, the massaging touch of his firm hand might have been excruciatingly pleasurable; now it was merely excruciating, as Cynthia smothered her cries in the pillow, trying to escape the torture but having nowhere to go. When he had finished, lifting her carefully, he laid her on top of its cool sheet.

She dozed on and off throughout the evening and night, awakening in a fever for more aspirin, in pain as the lotion was reapplied, in a start at the sound of puttering around the kitchen. As dazed as was her consciousness, she was grateful for the subtle reassurance of knowing Jonathan was there.

By the time she awoke in the morning, the fever had broken and she could think clearly again. It was very quiet—had Jonathan returned to his own cabin? Gingerly she eased herself to a sitting position and looked around. What a beautiful sight it was to her, that of his long body sprawled casually in sleep on the bunk next to hers. She momentarily forgot her discomfort as she gazed at him thus, totally at rest. So he had seen her through the night, exhausted as he must have been himself. The feelings that surged within her as she sat, undetected for once, looking at him, threatened to overwhelm her. She ached to lie down next to him, to fit her body to the contours of his, to feel the strength emanating from him . . . and to tell him of her love.

Yes, what she had earlier suspected, she now knew for sure. Mere gratitude for his presence last night could never account for the feelings that welled within her. More than anything, she yearned to give him everything she possessed.

But for now, she'd have to stick to bacon and eggs, she resigned herself, as she painstakingly maneuvered into a loose-fitting caftan and headed for the refrigerator.

CHAPTER FIVE

"Tell me, once more, what you remember," Jonathan had commanded later that morning, after he had properly scolded her for preparing breakfast and then suitably punished her by applying more medication to her sunburn.

She went over the incident again, scouring her memory for any new bit of information she might find. "Why is it so important?" she had asked him, puzzled by his fixation on the issue.

The look he gave her carried an odd mixture of concern and annoyance. "You were pretty sick last night, whether you knew it or not! I don't want it to happen again!"

"It was just a fluke, Jonathan," she shrugged off the episode, anxious to put it behind her.

A smile overspread his suddenly relaxed features. "So it's 'Jonathan' now, is it? Are we finally friends?"

She blushed and nodded. If he only knew, she mused. "Thank you for last night. It was nice to know you were here."

His eyes lit up in feigned surprise. "So you did know what was happening. If I'd known that . . ."

Before she could utter a word in denial, he stood up,

towering over her, barefooted as she was, took her face in his hands and kissed her lips ever so gently. Then he held her back at arm's length, his glimmering blue eyes penetrating hers, depriving her of breath. When he drew her to him once again, she raised her lips to his in subtle conveyance of all that could not yet be spoken. She offered him the warmth and openness that she felt inside; he reveled in it, devouring every last bit with his challenging kiss. It was only when he inadvertently slipped his muscular arm about her back and she flinched in pain, that their lips left one another's.

He spoke softly. "I'm going to change and then go for a swim. Maybe I can discover more about what happened to you yesterday. You stay here . . . out of the sun, please. I'll be back a little later to put on more lotion." With a light kiss to her turned-up nose, he left, the residual glow of his presence enveloping Cynthia in a cocoon of pleasure.

The pleasure lingered through the morning and into the afternoon, dulled only by the pain of her burn, the scarlet color of which had not yet begun to fade. Though the fever did not return, Cynthia didn't feel up to doing much of anything beside lounging stomach-down on the sofa.

She was unprepared for Jonathan's announcement when he walked into the lodge at midafternoon. There was a firm set to his jaw, a sternness in his voice that surprised her.

"Now I want you to listen to me and I don't want any arguments. I'm going in to Stonington to pick up our supplies and, yes," he held his hand out to still any interruption, "Suzanne will be coming back with me. You will be having dinner with us at my cabin tonight."

"I will not!" Instantly Cynthia rebelled, defying his order to the contrary. "I'm perfectly capable of making my own dinner!"

His voice softened. "I know that, but I want you to

meet Suzanne. She's a nice person. You might even like her."

"I can't believe you!" she exclaimed, shaking her head incredulously. "Are you that insensitive?"

His head shot up at her accusation and his eyes narrowed menacingly before softening again. "Yes, I'm aware of your feelings and I am aware of my own, although I wish like hell I weren't. Trust me, Cynthia. My relationship with Suzanne is not what you think."

" 'Trust me. Trust me'—that's ludicrous!" Pushed now by hurt, Cynthia bullheadedly argued with him. "How can I trust you when you won't be straightforward with me? I want to trust you," she pleaded, her anger quickly burning itself out as she added, more softly, "God knows I want to . . ." Her voice trailed off as she turned on her heel away from him.

Boldly, Jonathan walked right around to face her. "If it weren't for that damned sunburn, I'd show you a thing or two. But take my word for it. I'll be down here to get you at seven. Be ready or you'll be taken bodily . . . and I know how you feel about being humiliated in front of others," he taunted spitefully.

Lacking the strength to fight him any longer, Cynthia lowered her gaze to her hands which were tensely clasped in front of her. She was acutely aware of this man, with whom she was so madly in love, standing mere inches from her. Despite everything, she would always adore him!

Steel fingers pushed her chin up until her eyes met his. "It will work out, Cynthia." He spoke with such conviction that she had to believe him, insane as the whole situation seemed to her at that moment. His eyes skimmed her moist lips and he appeared torn, wanting to kiss her again yet holding back. It was Cynthia who made the decision for him, pulling away and heading for the kitchen area.

"I'll make a list of what I want," she sighed, as she balanced gingerly on the edge of a chair, pencil in hand and paper before her.

The dinner was a devastating personal experience for Cynthia, though she had no one to blame but herself. She was neither hungry nor companionable. Fortunately, she had her excuse, which she used repeatedly in apology for her behavior.

In hindsight, she had to admit that Suzanne was different than she had expected. Beautiful she was and stunningly dressed, but there was a natural, down-to-earth quality about her that seemed inconsistent with her ultrachic appearance. Jonathan had introduced her as one of his secretaries, yet Cynthia doubted how much secretarial work she actually did.

Also in hindsight, the relationship puzzled Cynthia more than ever. That Jonathan and Suzanne were fond of each other was obvious. They seemed well at ease and perfectly compatible. But lovers? There had been none of the nearness, the touching, the meaningful glances that would have implied such. Furthermore, Suzanne seemed totally unbothered by Cynthia's presence. There was not the slightest hint of jealousy in her demeanor, whereas Cynthia had to summon all her resources to hide her own. To make matters worse, Suzanne seemed anxious to befriend her, going out of her way to draw her into conversation.

By the time Jonathan suggested he walk her home, Cynthia was so ashamed of her own behavior in comparison with Suzanne's graciousness that she would have conceded the battle for Jonathan's sake alone. He deserved something better than her own churlishness.

They walked the short distance down the hill to Cynthia's cabin in silence. By this time, she ached both within and without, the latter from her sunburn and the clothes that chafed against it, the former from her jealousy and the love that fired it. It had been a bad twenty-four hours, she decided, as she opened the door and entered the cabin.

To her surprise and frustration, Jonathan had followed her right in. She whirled around to face him. "What is it?" she demanded crossly, tired, uncomfortable, and disgusted with herself.

Whatever he had had on his mind was put on the back burner when he saw the emotion on her face. He promptly crossed to the kitchen cabinet, took some aspirin and a glass of water, and quietly watched while she swallowed the pills.

"Get undressed so that I can put lotion on your back," he commanded firmly.

Her brown eyes opened wide in alarm. "I can do that. Don't you have somewhere to go?" she suggested acidly.

"When I'm done with you. Now, get undressed or I'll do it for you," he stated matter-of-factly.

Cynthia glared at the determination in his eyes for several moments before going into the bathroom to change into a robe. When she emerged, Jonathan took her arm and led her to the bed, whose cover he had already pulled back. He seated her forcefully, lowered himself behind her, pulled the robe from her shoulders and back, and proceeded to rub the lotion to the newly forming blisters before she could utter a word in protest. His hand felt so refreshingly cool against her burning skin, she had to admit, as she dropped her chin onto her chest.

"Wouldn't you be more comfortable without this?" he teased, lifting her bra strap slightly to medicate the area beneath it.

"You're the one who'd be more comfortable without it. But then, all you have to do is go back up the hill and you'll get all the comfort you want," she sneered.

Undaunted, Jonathan kept at his ministration. "You really are the bitch tonight, aren't you? Lie down."

Gingerly she followed his order and he applied the salve

to the backs of her legs and thighs, having roughly cast the robe completely aside, leaving her in her bra and panties. In another situation, she would have rebelled against this. Now, however, she was aware only of the welcome relief that the soothing lotion brought and the fatigue that was quickly flooding over her. She didn't remember saying good night to Jonathan, only the rustle of sheets as he lightly covered her and his comforting hand—were those his lips which brushed her forehead?—on hers.

Her recuperation was a longer process than Cynthia had anticipated. She still suffered from lingering spells of drowsiness and her back had blistered badly, making it difficult for her to sit for any length of time. Having reconciled herself to the idea of postponing work on her dissertation until she felt better, she made use of her time during the day to explore the island.

The smells of early summer enchanted her as she ambled down the hillside toward the southern end of the island, through a carpet of grasses, weeds, and wildflowers. With a black-eyed Susan tucked behind her ear, she admired the tangle of wild rose and the splash of flowering bayberry. She knelt to finger the small inverted bell blossoms, in masses of glorious bloom, which would, come August, provide blueberries for many a mouth-watering pie. She inhaled the fragrant scent of wild strawberries, tossing an occasional one in her mouth.

On another outing, she combed the amassed layers of upended rocks and boulders that guarded the northern tip of the island. Those higher up had maintained their craggy ruggedness, whereas those below the high-water mark were smoothed from years of beating by the cold pulse of the sea. She found the occasional indentation the perfect spot to take refuge from the exposure of the headland. From such dry and protected places she watched, mesmerized, as the waves pounded, roared, then built to explosive strength as a huge geyser erupted through a cleft in the rock, spewing water in all directions before retracing its eternal path back to the sea.

Of all the natural diversions the island had to offer, however, Cynthia's favorites were the three pines, themselves. Standing at the apex of the island, they provided a thick canopy under which she could linger to examine the beauty all around. The air here carried the tangy aroma of the woods, its lush collection of spruce, balsam, and hemlock a fitting audience for the regal pines that looked down from above.

This spot afforded a three-hundred-sixty-degree vista of breathtaking proportions. To the north was the light at Swan's Island, its beacon a homing signal for years; to the west was the mainland, attracting a congregation of boats and inspiring a cacophony of seagulls; to the south stood Isle au Haut and its neighboring islands, emerging specter-like from the frequently forming fog banks; to the east was the Atlantic, stretching endlessly before the eye, its color shifting with the weather, its temper following suit.

These leisure days, so novel for Cynthia, gave her time to think about all that had happened since her arrival on Three Pines. She had written off her sunburn as an unfortunate accident, born of imagination and exhaustion. What disturbed her more were the emotional upheavals taking place inside. The last thing she had expected when her uncle had proposed her summer on Three Pines was that she would fall in love. It had indeed happened; she could not turn back the clock. What remained to be seen was the future.

As much as she wished it were not so, the highlight of her days was seeing Jonathan. Hardly a day went by that she didn't see him. Throughout her convalescence he stopped by every evening, sometimes for dinner, sometimes just for coffee. Each Saturday, Suzanne appeared like clockwork; each Sunday, she was gone as regularly.

Cynthia was bewildered at how easily Jonathan made the transition from one companion to the next. In fact, there didn't seem to be any deterioration in his attitude toward her, even when Suzanne *was* around. Cynthia, herself, was the only one who became foul-tempered at these times, and if her moods bothered Jonathan, he never let it be known.

The main stumbling blocks in their relationship were the gaps that Jonathan persistently refused to fill in. And Cynthia was too much in love with him to risk his antagonism by pushing him beyond his limits. She resolved to be patient, believing instinctively that things would come to some sort of resolution before the summer was out.

She was deep in thought about Jonathan one afternoon as she stood against the tallest of the three pines, gazing out toward the open sea.

"So here you are," a low voice spoke behind her, startling her out of her reverie.

Her hand flew to her chest as she twirled around, gasping, "Oh! You frightened me, coming up the back way like that!" She blushed under his penetrating gaze, embarrassed at having been caught daydreaming about him.

His well-shaped lips broke into a broad grin. "You were miles away. Now what could have taken you that far away?" he teased. His hands were shoved into the pockets of his denims, and he looked so damned self-confident and terribly, terribly masculine that Cynthia could have screamed in frustration. Somehow she found herself tongue-tied.

"I . . . ah . . . I . . . it's so beautiful up here," she finally managed to spit out, but only after she had torn her eyes from his and looked back out at the ocean. "It's my favorite spot," she added, almost in a whisper. In these surroundings, Cynthia didn't know how long she would be able to keep her secret; she longed to tell Jonathan of her love for him, yet she dared not. She would have to restrain herself, she vowed silently. As fate would have it, it was not going to be easy.

Jonathan came up behind her and placed his hands on both of her arms, drawing his lean lines into contact with hers. Silently, he bent over and kissed the sensitive cord of her neck, sending an involuntary shudder reverberating through her lungs. Gently, his hands spread around her middle, his thumbs skimming her breasts ever so faintly, electrical in their feather touch. She closed her eyes at the pleasure of his closeness, crossing her arms over his to ensure their permanence. As he nibbled at her earlobe, she rested her head back against his shoulder, and his kisses moved to her throat with steadily increasing ardor.

"You smell so good," he murmured against her skin.

She was floating away in this heaven on earth and could only muster a faint, "Mmmm," as his lips continued their sensuous exploration.

He drew his head up and turned her within the circle of his arms until she faced him. "'Mmmm' . . . what does that mean?" he ventured huskily, the azure sparkles in his eyes shooting first to her own eyes then to her lips, moist and expectant, then back to her eyes, where they lingered endlessly, deciphering her message.

She couldn't hold back any longer. There was so much to say, so much to give; it was bursting within her and she couldn't confine it. Her arms went to the sinewy shoulders, fingertips on his rugged neck.

"Jonathan," she began softly, "I—I—" His finger against her lips silenced her momentarily until his lips took over. They drank of each other mutually—lips, teeth, tongue—all part of the impassioned interchange. She felt his response and knew then that his arousal had to be as mind-boggling as her own.

His hands roamed her back with a tenderness that belied their strength. His lips plundered hers, urgency quickening the pace for each of them. In a moment of abandon, he hugged her with a force that made her cry aloud, the blisters on her back not yet healed enough for such intense pressure.

His grip loosened immediately, though he made no move to release her completely. She reveled in the firmness of him, the raw masculinity that could have easily overpowered her. The huskiness in his voice confirmed what she had so vividly felt.

"I think I need a cold swim," he drawled quietly, his breath fanning over her in intoxicating nearness.

Arms still around his neck, Cynthia nodded in agreement. "I know you do," she grinned.

One eyebrow raised in feigned skepticism. "Now how would you know that?" He held her eyes, challenging her to respond.

She became momentarily cross at his persistence. "I do know some elementary biology." Strangely, she thought back, that Saturday night on the pier when Jonathan first kissed her and she had known of his arousal, she had been frightened. Now her body ached for his possession, total and unconditional. There was neither fear nor doubt; only such possession would satisfy the intense longings that tormented her. So it was not only Jonathan who needed a cold dunking, she mused. Uncannily, he read her thoughts.

With the blue flame in his eyes threatening to burn her, he crooned, "I think we could both use a cold swim. Do you feel up to it?" She smiled and nodded, grateful for his concern, and pleased at his suggestion. Suddenly he clasped her close to him, crushing her head against his chest, burying his own in her hair. His voice was thus muted when he spoke.

"So help me, I've a mind to take you, here and now, beneath these pines," he growled. Then he paused and released her. "Come on. Let's take that swim before we both do something we might regret."

Later that evening his words came back to her. No, she

would never regret his lovemaking. Even if it turned out that he was merely using her, taking advantage of her availability, that this was nothing but a summer fling on his part, she would always have her memories of him to savor, a very special part of her that would belong to him forever.

Tuesday

Dear Uncle William,

With the Fourth of July here and gone, I'm finally settling down to some serious work. It's not quite as easy as I thought it would be when I first arrived almost six weeks ago. The distractions here, though totally different from those in Philly, are just as frequent. For example, each change of weather demands one's full attention to appreciate it. For the most part, the days are warm and the evenings cool. It never really gets hot on the island, out here on the ocean, and, if anything, I've needed my heavier clothing more than I'd expected.

On those crisp sunny days, the water sparkles beneath an azure-blue sky. I see the distant islands, dotting the horizon like green jewels on a glittering necklace. My statistics can't compare in excitement with this view, Uncle William!

Thus, when the rains come, the sounds of the island take over where the view is dimmed. The patter of the heavy drops on my cabin, the rush of the wind through the dampened evergreens, the fierce pounding of the surf against the granite headland of the island—these sounds intermingle with the blast of the foghorn, the clang of the ship's bell, and the steady ring of the bell buoy. I wish you could hear it; it's a unique symphony.

Last week I had the weirdest experience yet. I

100

awoke to utter silence. No sound. No motion. Complete silence. It was frightening! At first, I thought my own senses had gone astray. Then I looked out to see that the island was shrouded in a thick bank of fog, blanketing everything from the shore to the top of the three pines with its heavy mist. How Jonathan found his way down here from his cabin I'll never know!

He has been wonderful, Uncle William. I do owe him an apology for having labeled him an "old miser," though I won't tell him if you don't! It's no wonder I can't get much work done, though. He is a distraction of the worst sort! But then, you know I wouldn't be saying this if I didn't enjoy every minute. He remains an enigma to me in many respects, but perhaps that's where the challenge comes in.

The evening of the Fourth, for example, was memorable. We took the yacht through Penobscot Bay into the harbor at Camden, from where we were able to watch the most magnificent display of fireworks I've ever seen. Down Easterners certainly do it right!

Geoffrey dropped me a note from Vermont; he sounds serious as usual, all business. Speaking of business again, I'm hoping to finish my statistical analyses this week; after that I'll only have the writing to do. I can hardly believe it! I'm grateful that I took your advice and contacted the library at Orono before I left; I'm planning to go there for one or two days this week.

Hope you're well, Uncle William. Keep those letters coming.

Your loving niece,
Cynthia

After Cynthia had sealed the letter, she thought back upon its contents. The fog. It had been an eerie, almost surrealistic happening. Yet, somehow, it symbolized her own experience this summer. Particularly with regard to her relationship with Jonathan, she felt as though she were within a fog, blanketed from a reality that lurked without. The times they spent together had a serenity, an unreality about them. Cynthia felt cushioned and protected here on the island with him, yet she knew that sooner or later the fog would lift. It was fear of what she would find, when it did, that gave her a sense of uneasiness which, try as she might to dispel it rationally, lingered naggingly in her subconscious.

Cynthia was right in one respect: There had been an overall tranquility to the summer. Fortunately for her peace of mind, she had not recognized it as the calm before the storm that it would prove to be. And she was totally unaware that the storm was about to break, as she set out for Orono and the State University the following Wednesday.

Jonathan had given her no argument when she announced her plans several days earlier. He had even offered to take her to Stonington early on Wednesday morning. However, his mood took her by surprise when he showed up for breakfast beforehand.

"Do you know where the library is?" he demanded gruffly over the rim of his coffee cup.

"Yes, I got complete directions before I left Philly. Are you sure you can do without me for two days?" she teased, scrubbing the remnants of scrambled eggs from the frying pan.

The sharpness of his answer startled her. "I've done very well without you for a hell of a long time and I'm sure I'll continue to do so," he snarled menacingly as he shoved his chair back and stalked away from the table.

She glanced at him inquisitively, puzzled by his sudden bad temper, but the broad expanse of muscular back told her nothing. Shrugging her shoulders, she mumbled, half

102

to herself, "Sorry. . . ." and she finished cleaning the dishes.

During the boat ride into Stonington, he made an effort to be pleasant, but Cynthia could see that something was on his mind.

"What's the matter, Jonathan?" she finally dared to ask as the harbor closed in around them.

His eyes shot to her face before he was able to control them. "Why would anything be the matter?" he returned coolly.

"You just seem . . . annoyed with me." Her eyes held his, searching for a clue but finding none.

He looked away from her toward the town lying over the bow. "I have some business matters on my mind. Some calls to make while I'm here," he mumbled, his eyes clouded with thought.

Dissatisfied, Cynthia pursued the matter further. "Without sounding too naive, I thought that that was one of Suzanne's jobs."

His head turned toward her, his expression fiercely threatening. "I take care of my own business. Never forget that," he boomed, then added in a lower, though equally as venomous, tone, "And my own affairs have nothing to do with you!"

Cynthia shrank back, stung sharply by his antagonism. She made no other attempt at conversation, and their parting at the dock in Stonington was a civil, perfunctory matter.

"I'll be here tomorrow evening around seven to meet you," he informed her distantly, before he headed in the direction of the post office, with neither an offer to see her to her car, nor any word of good-bye. She stood in amazement for several moments, giving him enough of a lead so that she would not appear to be following, even though her car was garaged in the same direction as the one he had taken. She was totally bewildered by his behavior. The past weeks had been so delightful; Jonathan had been attentive and charming—yes, affectionate and even passionate on more than one occasion. She had dared to hope that he might begin to see her as she now saw him, as the person with whom she could spend the rest of her life. His behavior toward her today shattered that delusion, leaving her of heavy heart as she drove out of Stonington.

To her surprise, considering the dull ache inside her, Cynthia felt good to be at the wheel of her Chevy again. Only now, as she passed through town after town, did she realize how close she had stayed to the island since she had arrived six weeks ago. Not that she had minded a minute of it . . . as long as there was the hope of seeing Jonathan each day.

By midmorning, she arrived in Orono, headed straight for the library, and went right to work. The hours she spent were productive ones, but by evening, when she checked into the only hotel in town and sat down for dinner, she was tired.

Returning to her small room, she piled her papers neatly by her overnight bag, opting to arise first thing the next morning to compensate for any lost time this evening. Somehow she knew that she wouldn't be able to accomplish much now. Her mind had begun to wander. Hoping to relax, she took a walk through the center of the university town, browsing in bookstores, window-shopping, almost tempted to take in a movie as a diversion, though knowing that it wouldn't hold her concentration.

Her heart ached at the thought of Jonathan. What motivated his reactions to her? What did he feel for Suzanne? What did he mean about his relationship with her being different than it appeared? How could that be, when they shared the same cabin every Saturday night? There were times when Cynthia could believe that Jonathan loved her—a look in his eye, a tone in his voice, a tremor of emotion coursing through his body when he held her close. But her reasoning told her that he was merely burning the candle at both ends, using her when Suzanne was not on the island. It was her own heart, her own imagination, her own desire that had misread his advances, and now she would be the one to suffer.

So deep in thought was she that she didn't realize she had reached a corner and stepped off the curb and into the street until the terrifying sound of a fast-approaching motor shocked her into awareness. She looked up into the oncoming headlights, blinding in their brilliance, and was momentarily frozen in place, unable to move forward or back.

By some miraculous quirk of fate, a fellow pedestrian rounded the corner at that moment and yelled, "Get out of the way! Move!," giving her the needed momentum to rush across to the other side and barely escape the vehicle's winding path.

"Are you all right?" the young man asked, rushing to where Cynthia had sunk down on the curbstone.

She looked up into the concerned eyes of a good-looking, dark-haired fellow, clad in cut-offs and a T-shirt, and barefooted. He fit perfectly into the image of the summer student in the university town.

Stunned, but otherwise fine, she answered him. "Yes, thank you. I appreciated your yell—I was paralyzed out there."

"I don't blame you. That guy was bearing down pretty fast." He shook his head in disgust. "Must have been drunk or something. Crazy driver! You sure you're okay?" he asked a final time, as he helped her to her feet.

"I'm sure!" she smiled, and she really was, thanks to him.

"Better be careful to look both ways," he called over his shoulder as he was off, adding as an afterthought, "and especially watch out for blue vans!"

Cynthia headed directly back to her hotel, none the

worse for wear, though steeped in self-reproachment at having been so careless. It would have served her right, she concluded, as she headed for a hot tub, to be punished for her obsession with Jonathan. Forget about the man, she pleaded with herself. Yield to the inevitable. Let Suzanne have him!

But then, Suzanne had him already! And his attitude toward her this morning should have convinced her that he didn't want any part of Cynthia, except perhaps for the one part she was reluctant to give. It was the continual ache inside, both for need of his love and want of his passion, which kept her awake for most of the night.

Her mind conjured up image after image of Jonathan, one more torturously appealing than the next. First, he was standing on the yacht, the wind whipping his tawny hair back from his forehead, molding his clothes more intimately to his frame. Then he lay on the sandy beach, his bronzed chest, firm and virile, awaiting her touch, his lean torso made all the more attractive by his thin swimsuit.

She tossed from one side to the other on her bed in vain efforts to erase these pictures. But with the demise of one a new one cropped up, invariably more heartbreaking than the image it had replaced. The final fragment Cynthia remembered, before falling into a fitful sleep, was the sight of Jonathan, standing erect beneath the three pines, his body held as regally, as confidently, as victoriously as those of the trees. He was a survivor, just like the three; he would always continue to grow, leaving so much of mortality far behind.

Exhausted as she was when her alarm clock rang the next morning—what a contrast to the island, she noted, where the bright and cheery alarm that nature provided was its earliest riser, the sun—Cynthia dressed, breakfasted, and buried herself in the library before she might have time to reconsider spending the day there. But this would be her final chance to check on this last research before returning to the island.

Returning to the island . . . her stomach fluttered madly at the thought. How odd to think she'd been away a mere twenty-four hours; it seemed more like days since she'd seen Jonathan. By the time she was ready to call it quits at five, she had just about given up on the idea of pushing him out of her mind. It was with barely bridled excitement that she drove back toward Stonington.

CHAPTER SIX

Cynthia had agreed to meet Jonathan on the pier at seven. But, having run into an accident that tied up traffic for a good fifteen minutes, it was a little later when she pulled in to the Baileys' driveway and parked her car. Hurriedly, motivated on the one hand by eagerness to see Jonathan and on the other by fear of his wrath at her tardiness, she ran down the side street, proceeding as quickly as she could with her notebook and papers in one arm and her overnight case and pocketbook slung over the other shoulder and banging bulkily at her hip with each step.

Breathlessly, she rounded the last corner onto the main street and it was only when she bounded off the curb in a beeline to the pier that she heard the gunning of an engine. For an instant she was frozen, mesmerized by a sense of déjà vu, of having experienced this same trauma once before; it was a subconscious feeling of panic, all too familiar.

A sharp pain in her elbow brought her back to reality, a sense of being thrown, then a broader pain in her side, as the breath was knocked out of her. When she finally regained it and her bearings, she was resting against the side of the building with which she had collided, driven there by the impact of the vehicle's sideswiping of her. She was aware of people pushing to her aid, of her papers and bags scattered nearby, and then of the group being eased aside by an ashen-faced Jonathan Roaman.

He knelt down beside her, his back to the crowd, his face infinitely close to hers. "My God, are you hurt?" he asked, an anxiety in his voice that Cynthia had never heard before. Dazed, she looked up at him, his sandy hair windblown, his chest rising and falling with the uneven beat of alarm. Oh, God, she thought, she loved him so; she could overcome any hurt if only he could love her in return. He took her shoulders very gently, repeating, "Cynthia, are you hurt?"

She shook her head. "No . . . no. I think I'm all right." She had intended her voice to be forceful, yet it came out sounding strangely weak and not at all like her own. She made a move to stand up, but his hands became firm and held her down.

"Don't move yet. Do you feel any pain?" he demanded, the anxiety having been replaced by the firm commanding which she more easily recognized.

Cynthia concentrated on her body. "My elbow—it hurts badly, but that's all." She seemed to be having trouble focusing on just what had happened. Suddenly she looked up at him. "My papers. Where are they?" She began to look frantically around her until Jonathan's low growl stopped her.

"How can you be so concerned about those damned papers at a time like this? They're right over there," he added, pointing to where several of the villagers were gathering her things together. "Your papers will survive. I'm more worried about you. Sit still for a minute more," he ordered as he proceeded, with the thoroughness of a medic and the gentleness of a lover, to feel her every limb for any sign of broken bones. At her elbow, she grimaced in pain. Her gaze met his at the huge gash there, which was now bleeding profusely. Whipping a clean handkerchief from his pocket, Jonathan bound the elbow as tightly as he dared, unsure both of the state of the bone and the state of Cynthia's pain tolerance, already pushed to its extreme.

"Can you stand up?" he asked softly, putting his hands under her arms and lifting her to her feet. His eyes followed her face, watching for signs of undiscovered pains and, seeing that there were none, he crooned gently by her ear, "Now, I want you to walk. We're going down the block and around the corner to the doctor's house. He's an old friend—Dr. Moreland. He's sure to be there at this hour. Can you make it? I could carry you . . ."

"No!" Cynthia refused emphatically, embarrassed by the attention of the onlookers and determined to convince Jonathan she was stronger than he thought.

Guiding her next to him, they walked slowly to the doctor's house, a small, cape-style house surrounded by a freshly painted picket fence. Sure enough, the doctor was at home, just finishing his dinner.

"No, no, my boy . . . come right in," he insisted firmly to silence Jonathan's apologies. "I certainly don't need that second strawberry shortcake!" he chuckled. He was a tall, robust man who reminded Cynthia immediately of her uncle. As he questioned her over his wire-rimmed spectacles about the accident itself, she felt an immediate trust in him, answering his queries as well as she possibly could, considering that it had happened so fast she could remember little.

He led them through the house to his office at the rear, where he proceeded to examine Cynthia for broken bones and other injuries, much as Jonathan had. His examination was to be much more thorough, and Cynthia was relieved when he asked Jonathan to wait in the outer room. She fa-

110

vored her elbow as she eased out of her clothes, doubtful as to the necessity of this degree of thoroughness—until she saw the purple welts running the length of her side, practically from armpit to hip. The skin had barely broken, but it was evident that she would feel more discomfort as time went on. There were other minor bruises, but the probing of her abdomen and chest revealed no broken ribs or internal injuries, and as he helped her dress, Dr. Moreland pronounced her a very fortunate young lady.

"Let's get Jonathan in here," he suggested when she had finished buttoning her blouse. "I know how impatient he can get," he added with a twinkle in his eye that made Cynthia smile for the first time since the accident.

"Have you known Jonathan long?" she asked, intrigued by the apparent familiarity.

"For quite a few years now. His parents and I were close friends. I've patched him up myself any number of times," he grinned as he opened the door and motioned for Jonathan to rejoin them.

"What's the verdict, Henry?" he asked, all the while looking at Cynthia.

"Well, my boy, she's a very lucky girl, as I just told her. Some bruises and scrapes, but the elbow is the only thing that needs any attention. It needs to be stitched. I'll drive you over to the medical center so that we can get it X rayed at the same time. I want to rule out a chipped bone."

It was as though Cynthia were a mere spectator in this and the events that followed. The two men seemed to have taken over completely. Although one part of her protested, the other was grateful, in her still somewhat dazed state, to leave the arrangements to them.

They were met at the medical center by a technician who both took the X rays and assisted the doctor in taking the necessary stitches. Fortunately the pictures showed no broken bones, but Dr. Moreland insisted on profusely bandaging the gash, thereby minimizing the movement her elbow might make.

Through the entire process, Jonathan stood nearby, alternately looking at Cynthia, then her arm, then back to her face for any sign of the strain having caught up with her. Cynthia, herself, was surprised that there was very little. She still felt stunned and thereby protected from the full impact of her accident and the fate which she had miraculously escaped. Physically, she likewise felt numb, her arm having been anesthetized locally while the stitches were taken. It was only as they prepared to leave the medical center that she began to feel the throbbing from her other bruises.

Rather than relaxing under the steady reassurances of Dr. Moreland, Jonathan seemed to become more anxious. When he finally walked Cynthia to the car and deposited her in the middle of the front seat, he spoke softly to her.

"I want to ask Henry one or two questions. I'll be right back. Okay?"

Feeling suddenly tired, she merely nodded and lay her head back against the seat, closing her eyes as she did so. But her mind was conscious enough to overhear the conversation that took place on the steps of the center, not far from the car.

"I'm worried about her, Henry. She's usually so full of fight. She hasn't said 'boo' once. Is she really all right?" Even from where she sat, Cynthia detected the same anxiety she had heard in his voice earlier. Was he really worried about her, or was it just his sense of responsibility toward her, she couldn't help wondering.

Dr. Moreland explained in his low, even voice. "It's very normal, Jon. She's in a kind of shock. It'll hit her, don't worry. Will someone be with her?"

Cynthia waited for the response but heard none. The doctor went on, in a softer voice that she could just barely make out. "Is this it, Jon?" Again, no response. She felt her heart beating faster. There was something odd in this one-sided conversation; what was it really about? "Guard it, my boy!" the doctor added. She heard footsteps approaching the car and the two men got in on either side of her.

"Guard it," he had said. Guard what? What were they talking about? It was as though Jonathan and the doctor had completely switched subject matter, and evidently this had little to do with her. She promptly pushed their words to the back of her mind and concentrated on the drive. This turned out to be a difficult feat, with her body aching on one side from the accident and on the other from the feel of Jonathan's body next to her, his thigh rubbing against hers with every turn the car took. It must have been pure escapism that knocked her out, for the next thing she knew, her head was nestled against Jonathan's chest, his arm was curled protectively around her shoulder, and his other hand was against her cheek, gently waking her.

"We're here, Cynthia," he whispered in her ear. "Let's get to the boat. Can you make it?" His nearness was the shot of adrenaline she needed to shake off her grogginess and ease out of the car after him.

Dr. Moreland leaned his head toward them. "Let me know if there's any problem. If not, I'll see you next week!" he called, and he drove off toward his home.

"Where are my papers?" Cynthia asked, suddenly remembering the belongings that had been left at the scene of the accident.

Jonathan stopped short in his tracks and glared at her. "Damn it! Is that all you have on your mind?"

Cynthia returned his stare silently. The anger she saw now was an echo of that which he had expressed yesterday morning before she had left for Orono. It hurt her far more than any of this physical discomfort, and the latter was rapidly increasing. Suddenly, the world seemed to be

113

falling about her, and a deep anguish churned her insides. The harsh reality of the accident came to her, and she had to gather every bit of strength to reply to Jonathan.

"No," she whispered, moving slowly away from him toward the boat. In that instant, she didn't care a whit about her work, her pocketbook, or her overnight bag. She just didn't want to think . . . about anything.

Jonathan strode ahead of her to the boat, leaving her to climb aboard herself. As soon as she had entered the cockpit, he released the lines, started the motor, and headed for Three Pines. He gave her not a glance as she sat, huddled in misery, on one of the bunks.

It was a silent ride, not a word spoken between them. Only the engine roared; the same engine that Cynthia had recalled droning steadily now seemed to be the outlet for Jonathan's unspoken fury.

They docked at Three Pines and Cynthia followed Jonathan up onto the pier, where he secured the boat and then turned to her.

"Wait here a minute," he ordered coldly, reentering the boat and emerging moments later with her notebook, purse, and bag all on one arm. "Let's go!" he said, propelling her forward with a firm hand on her shoulder, effectively erasing the look of surprise on her face at the appearance of her things.

Cynthia felt herself stretched taut. She was tired, hurting, and becoming increasingly resentful of his attitude toward her. How could he vacillate so, she wondered, from all care and tenderness one moment to harsh anger and roughness the next. He was pushing her now physically and emotionally. How long could he expect her to hold up?

Perhaps that was what he wanted to do—to break her and establish his own dominance. Well, she vowed, she would resist, as long as there was an ounce of strength left in her! Lifting her chin and straightening her shoulders, she pulled out of his grasp and headed toward the path leading to her cabin.

Within an instant, her hand had been seized and she was being pulled in another direction. "You're coming this way," he growled over his shoulder as he pulled her up the hill toward his own house.

"But—"

"You're staying at my place tonight. There's more room," he roared menacingly. Why he wanted her near when he disliked her so, Cynthia could not understand. She furthered her protest by pulling in the opposite direction, but she was promptly yanked forward, and the streak of pain that shot through her body quelled all further thought of rebellion.

Safely seeing her into the cabin, he kicked the door shut, dropped her things on a large leather chair, and finally released her hand before he turned to light a fire in the fireplace. Cynthia made her way to the far end of the cabin, overlooking the ocean, where she stood at mute attention, unsure as to what to do next. To her pleasant surprise, the sight of the island and this beautiful oceanic panorama warmed her. It was indeed good to be home!

Home? But it wasn't her home. It was Jonathan's home. And she would never see it again, once this summer was over. A new ache joined the others, wiping out the momentary pleasure that the island had given her.

A loud voice boomed angrily in her ear. "Now, I want you to tell me exactly what happened."

Cynthia whirled round to face Jonathan, her brown eyes widened in fear at his tone of voice. "What do you mean?" she asked softly, chiding herself for her timidity.

"I want to know how that accident happened," he continued relentlessly.

Puzzled, she searched his fiery blue eyes. "But you heard me tell Dr. Moreland . . ."

"I want you to tell *me* what happened," he interrupted.

115

"Everything you can remember. Now!" His voice was louder than ever, his jaw tensed visibly, and she shrank involuntarily from his penetrating eyes.

Cynthia turned her back on him, her stomach churning. What was wrong with him? He was glaring at her malevolently. What had she done to offend him so? She could find no answers to these questions. Nor did she have the time to search, for he grabbed her shoulders and forced her back to face him.

"Now!" he growled, narrow-eyed and thin-lipped, and she dared not evade him again.

Slowly, deliberately, and with much mental pain, she retold the little she could, placing the blame where she felt it belonged, squarely on her own shoulders. She looked away as she concluded, "It was my own carelessness. That's all." It was when she began to move away from Jonathan that a terrifying thought jolted her to the core. She completely forgot about him, standing a mere few feet away, as she whispered, "My God, twice in as many days . . ."

There was a long silence, during which Cynthia tried to assimilate this new realization. She had never been accident prone before. Never! Now, suddenly two potentially dangerous incidents—one right after the other. And there was that terrible sunburn. She realized then that she was in the middle of something which she didn't understand—and she found herself on the verge of panic.

"What did you say?" his low voice cut through the whirlpool that threatened to envelop her. She was unable to speak, so great was the shock of what she was thinking. "What did you say?" he repeated, more loudly this time, simultaneously grabbing her shoulders and shaking her to her senses. But, what could she say to Jonathan? That none of these accidents had, in fact, been accidents? That someone wanted to harm her? He'd think her crazy . . . or would he? Maybe he knew something that she didn't! She just couldn't cope any more.

116

She had to get away, had to think. A fit of trembling overtook her and she turned pale. She only knew that she had to leave. With surprising strength, she tore herself out of his grasp and headed for the door. She had to escape, to be alone, to straighten things out in her mind.

As she reached the door, two broad hands flattened thunderously against it, preventing her leaving, indeed preventing her movement out of their confines. She lay her forehead against the door in defeat, suddenly too tired to fight, overwhelmed with fear and confusion, trembling uncontrollably.

Deliberately, the hands lowered to her shoulders and slowly turned her around. Cynthia could feel the warmth of his body, straight and powerful before her. She felt the strength of his thighs pressing against hers, intensifying her turmoil. She lowered her head, knowing that he could feel her shaking but wanting to hide from him the tears which were fast gathering at her eyelids. A commanding grip took her chin, forcing it up against her will. She shut her eyes in a final attempt to salvage this last bit of dignity.

"Look at me, Cynthia," he demanded quietly, with a gentleness in his words to temper the order.

As she opened her eyes, her fragile composure crumbled. Tears spilled freely onto her cheeks and her knees threatened to buckle under the violent tremors that shook her.

Then, at the moment when she most needed it, she was drawn into the circle of his arms, her head pressed against his chest, her tears dampening his shirt. Jonathan held her, one hand caressing her back, another smoothing her hair.

"It's all right, honey," he crooned. "Let it all come out." His mouth was against her hair, his breathing warming her. Slowly, her arms crept around him, then held on as for her life.

Her sobs came freely, uncontrollably, expressing the anguish of the day that had just been. It was his own heartbeat, steady against her ear, which eventually calmed her, sobs giving way to intermittent tears, finally yielding to occasional short gasps.

Cynthia felt herself being lifted off her feet into Jonathan's arms. Instinctively, her own arms went over his shoulders and she buried her face in his neck. She cared not where he was taking her, only that he not let her go. She needed him desperately, she realized; never had she needed anyone as she needed Jonathan now. She needed his warmth to drive off the chill in her bones, his strength to compensate for her lack of it, his comfort to assuage her mental torment. Please help me, Jonathan, she begged silently, the force of her arms around his neck her only source of communicating this plea.

He carried her toward the fireplace, easing her down onto the pillows that lay in heaps before it. Then he joined her, cradling her, holding her close, such that they could watch the fire, side by side. He spoke not a word, but periodically looked down at her or reached over to smooth a stray hair away from her tearstained cheek.

Thinking back on these moments in the days to come, Cynthia would be repeatedly astonished by the workings of the human brain. For, she successfully blotted out all of the negative things she had felt so vividly short minutes before, aware only of the nearness of Jonathan, of the understanding he gave her wordlessly, of the ever steady beat of his heart which, like the eternal pulse of the sea itself, stood as a reminder that life went on.

Bidden by a sixth sense, she lifted her head from his chest to meet his gaze. She was totally unprepared for the tenderness she found there, and once again, but for a completely different reason, tears welled over her long brown lashes. There was so much she wanted to say, but words eluded her.

Jonathan's eyes caressed her every feature, his thumb diverted a falling tear; then, with a fierceness strangely en-

118

hanced by gentleness, he pulled her head against him once more, smothering her in the circle of his arms until she emitted a long, intermittently hiccuping, sigh of peace.

"Feel better?" he asked softly, his voice velvet smooth in an intimate, though nonseductive way.

She nodded against him. "Uh-huh." Remarkably, she did feel better. Nothing had changed; the facts remained. Strange and mysterious, they continued to unsettle her. But all of this became irrelevant as long as Jonathan held her. She would cope later. For now, she wanted nothing more than the sanctuary of his arms. It was within this aura of security that she fell asleep, the fire crackling before her, its flames vital and passionate, mirroring the man whose body cradled hers.

She awoke several times during the night, each time with recurrent visions of her mishaps, one or another or an imagined new one. In each instance, when she bolted up, Jonathan was there to hold and soothe her, calmly assuring her of his presence.

When dawn finally sent its pale blue beacon through the large windows of the cabin, Cynthia awoke to find that, the fire having burned out, she was warmly covered by a heavy quilt, tucked around her in swaddling fashion.

It took her several moments to remember where she was. Slowly the events of the previous day filtered into her consciousness, her stiff and aching body confirming them. Where was Jonathan, she wondered in alarm. Carefully, pampering her stitched elbow, she turned over to look for him—to find herself within inches of his wide open blue eyes.

How long he had been watching her she had no way of knowing. He was resting on his bent elbow, a hand supporting his head. And he smiled when she saw him, warming her heart as no quilt ever could.

"How did you sleep?" he asked gently, his smile lingering, softening his features in a heart-rending way.

Cynthia lay her head back on the pillow as she regarded him, returning his smile. "Fine," she replied, choosing to ignore the nightmares that had tortured her.

"We both know that's a lie," he accused mildly, assuming from her looks that she felt better and could handle his banter. "But," and he held out his hand to silence her coming protest, "that's water over the dam. You'll have plenty of time to rest today."

As he spoke, Cynthia studied his face with such intensity that his words floated over her. God, he is handsome, she marveled. Even with a day's growth of beard, a disheveled headful of hair, a wrinkled shirt and jeans, he looked sensuously appealing.

Reading her thoughts, he leaned over and touched her lips with his, sampling their sweetness as one would a delicate French pastry. She returned his play, shy at first for reasons that puzzled her. His overwhelming physical appeal soon eliminated any hesitance, however, and Cynthia found herself reciprocating with nips and licks in echo of his.

"It's best in the morning, you know," Jonathan murmured huskily against her lips, still the only point of their bodies which touched.

"I wouldn't know about that," she whispered, even as she felt the stirrings deep within, in growing demand for his touch.

He pulled himself away and stood up. "You will," he concluded, eyes twinkling. As he looked down at her, scanning her length, the fire of a smoldering passion in his gaze, Cynthia knew that, if there were many more nights like the last, he would be right.

She started to stand, but doubled over in pain before she had achieved her goal. Instantly, Jonathan was at her side, easing her back down onto the pillows.

"Damn it, Cynthia. You have to be careful. Is it very

120

painful?" he questioned her, noting the beads of sweat that had appeared on her brow.

She shook her head, breathing deeply. "N-no. I just didn't e-expect the soreness," she stammered, avoiding his gaze. It wouldn't do for her to be an invalid for several days, she thought apprehensively.

Jonathan spoke quietly, her pallor convincing him of her need for assurance. "Look, honey, I'm going to put on some coffee and make breakfast. You had no dinner last night, did you?" Acknowledging her shaking head, he went on. "Then I'm going to run a bath for you and you'll sit in it for a nice long time, if you know what's good for you."

"But my arm," she interrupted, looking questioningly up at him. "I can't get it wet . . ."

"That's a damned stupid statement coming from a professor," he snapped impatiently. "Obviously, you'll keep your elbow out of the water," he explained, delivering each word separately, ridiculing her, "and if you can't, I'll stay there and hold it up for you."

She looked sharply at him. "I can manage." She could very easily do without his wisecracks.

"Now, you rest while I get to work. I'll bring up some things from your cabin later."

"Jonathan," she began, raising herself up slightly to emphasize her point, "wouldn't it be much easier if I simply went back there myself? I can rest as easily there."

"No." The command was firm. "You'll stay here. I want to keep a close eye on you. And, you know, you're not off the hook yet. I intend to get my complete explanation later. Now, lie down!"

"Jonathan, I—" she started to protest, but her words were cut short by his sudden fury.

"That's enough, Cynthia," he fumed, as he pressed her shoulders down onto the pillows again, with only the smattering of resistance that her weakened muscles could offer. The look in his eyes frightened her. "You have had two

121

serious accidents now," he seethed, "not to mention whatever else happened that you didn't see fit to tell me. If I'm going to be a nursemaid, I'll sure as hell do it right. Now stay put and keep still or, so help me, I'll strip every bit of clothing from your body and then you won't dare go anywhere, will you?" His eyes taunted her, and before she knew it, her own hand had swung up to deliver a firm slap to his cheek. But her reflexes had been slowed by the physical ordeal, and he caught her wrist before it had reached its mark.

To her horror, he swung over to straddle her body, immobilizing her, while his hands moved to her blouse and began unbuttoning buttons, making good his threat. Defensively she clawed at his arms, squirming frantically beneath his weight.

"No, Jonathan. Please, no," she begged, tears of humiliation filling her eyes. "I'll do as you say. Please—don't." Her hands gripped his wrists, and she was acutely aware of the pain in her elbow and the dull ache all over.

Her blouse lay completely open now, her lace-edged bra the only barrier between her heaving breasts and his appreciative eye. A final agonized "Nooo . . ." escaped her lips as his hands came to rest on the snap of her jeans. She looked away, defeated, too weak to resist.

"Will you do as I say?" his low voice gloated.

She nodded without looking at him, her eyes shut in embarrassment.

"I didn't hear you," he taunted, his hands moving against her bare stomach, about to resume their punishment. "Will you do as I say?"

"Yes," she whispered almost inaudibly, her face still averted. A steel vise gripped her chin, forcing her to look at him.

"Now tell *me*. Will you do as I say," He glared down at her triumphantly, and if it weren't for fear of retaliation, Cynthia would have spit in his eye.

Instead, she merely stared at him as long and defiantly as she dared, before uttering a begrudging, "Yes," whereupon his hands reversed their activity until she was properly dressed once more. Then, to her utter surprise, he gathered her to him, hugging her warmly for a moment before he kissed her forehead and gently lay her down.

"That's my good girl," he smiled, pushing her hair back from her face as he rose and headed for the kitchen.

CHAPTER SEVEN

Later that morning, at Jonathan's prodding, she timidly told him of the near miss she had had in Orono. Jonathan became furious, intimidating her all the more.

"What kind of car was it?" he demanded.

"I don't know . . . it happened too fast . . . just like last night."

He persisted impatiently. "But certainly you remember something, Cynthia. Size—big? Small? What color?"

She shook her head in confusion. "I just don't . . . wait . . ." Suddenly she remembered the parting words of the student who had come to her aid that first time. "A blue van—I think it was a blue van." She raised questioning eyes to Jonathan's.

He brooded, looked out toward the ocean, struggling with some inner dilemma. His jaw clenched and unclenched alternately with his fists. He said nothing.

"Why is that so important?" Cynthia asked. "It's a little late to catch him!" Still Jonathan glared out the window.

"Maybe not," he muttered softly under his breath. Then he turned and began pacing the floor, deep in thought.

Cynthia broke into it with her suggestion. "Should we go to the police?"

"No!" he barked with a ferocity that startled her, then he softened immediately. "That is, not yet. Let me handle this." And he continued his brooding from the large leather chair before the fireplace.

Cynthia followed him. "I don't know why you're taking this all so seriously," she began, rationalizing for her own benefit as well as for his. "It was just coincidence, that's all. And my own carelessness . . .'"

"Two blue vans?" His words, combined with the icy stare he turned on her, sent a shock through her.

"W-what?"

"You heard me . . . it was a blue van that hit you last night, too. Is that still a coincidence?" he growled, his blue eyes boring into her.

This time it was Cynthia who needed a seat. She sank down in the deck chair by the small Parsons table on the opposite side of the fireplace from where Jonathan sat. Staring at the cold ashes of last night's fire, she attempted to understand what was happening. But, try as she might, she could barely make any sense out of the mess in which she found herself.

Ironic, she thought, how she had expected this summer to be idyllic. Yet, look at her now, dwelling in utter confusion. She was tormented by mystery, those uneasy feelings and unanswered questions which had presented themselves even before she had left Philadelphia. Why had Jonathan Roaman wanted a "house-sitter" to begin with? Why had he been in touch with John Cummings of the DEA, who had in turn contacted her uncle? Did Jonathan's deep interest in the drug situation along the coast have something to do with the DEA? Did she dare ask him?

Then there were the accidents. Did they have any connection with one another? First there was the sunburn; could there have been some reason for her having passed

125

out for four hours on the sand, other than exhaustion? If so, what? What had she, in fact, banged her leg against, out in the waves? Then there were the two vehicle mishaps, the one in Orono which had been nothing but a close call, and the second in Stonington which had resulted in a gashed elbow and multiple black-and-blue marks. Two blue vans, Jonathan had said. It was a terrifying thought that some mysterious person or persons, for equally as mysterious reasons, were out to get her!

And, finally, amidst all the turmoil, here she sat, deeply in love with the man on the other side of the fireplace. At the scene of last night's accident, he had accused her, she recalled wryly, of thinking first and foremost of her papers and bags; little had he known that the first thing on her mind when he rushed to her was how very much she loved him! It was the very joy of seeing his face again, after less than two days apart from him, which had initially numbed her senses to all else.

What was the outcome of all this turmoil to be, she wondered, as she saw Jonathan stir from his own trance and walk toward the window once more. Would she ever have the answers to the questions that assailed her? Were these accidents only a beginning? Did she dare stay here? Did she dare leave? And what about her love for Jonathan—was there to be any future for it?

At that moment, Jonathan approached her, his form tense, his blue eyes overclouded. He stared at her for several moments, untold thoughts filtering through his mind, his expression unfathomable to Cynthia, who had interrupted her own agonizing to await his move.

"I'll be back." It could have been the eleventh commandment, for the force and authority it conveyed, as his statement thundered down to her with its awesome strength.

"Where are you going?" Cynthia cried in alarm, spurred on by a combination of curiosity and anxiety. As Jonathan headed for the door, she jumped from her seat, grateful that his back was to her and he was thus unable to see the expression of pain on her face at her quick movement. The hot bath earlier had been soothing and relaxing, but her tension now counteracted it, further aggravating the muscles that had been bruised.

"Where are you going?" she repeated from the door, now yelling after the figure that had already merged into the wooded haven of the hillside. "Damn . . ." she swore under her breath, knowing that the answer to this particular question would have to wait until he returned. Going to the window, she watched as the yacht moved slowly away from the pier, headed south, then gradually disappeared from sight around the tip of the island.

It had been just after noon that Jonathan had left. The bright sun of the early morning had yielded to overcast skies by then, and the rain began in earnest by midafternoon with still no sign of his return. Cynthia remained in his cabin, too drained to attempt much physically and not quite ready to test Jonathan's temper by returning to her own cabin. As he had promised, he brought some of her things to her after breakfast, including the terry robe which he had insisted she wear after her bath.

Restless, more psychologically than physically, Cynthia whiled away the time by wandering around the cottage. She found herself longingly fingering the things that Jonathan would touch in the course of a day: the chrome and black fireplace tools, the dark brown Formica Parsons table, the teak and ivory chess set on the coffee table, the sparkling white kitchen countertop.

She moved aimlessly about, glancing out the window every now and then to see whether the boat had returned to the pier, and, seeing that it hadn't, directed her attention to some other diversion.

Purely by chance, she noticed the closed door of the

spare room. What was inside? Jonathan had never invited her into the room, although he had moved freely in and out of it in her presence. Would he mind if she went in herself? Overcome by curiosity, she timidly reached for the door handle, half expecting it to be locked. It was with surprise that she felt the knob turn easily in her hand and a gentle push against the knotty pine revealed to her a good-sized room, ceilinged almost entirely with skylights, which provided the only outside light entering the room.

The walls, made of the rustic pine she easily recognized, were largely laden with built-in shelves, carrying an assortment of books, trophies, interesting stone carvings, and pieces of scrimshaw. There were two studio beds, arranged end to end along the outside wall. But the most compelling feature of the room was the imposing oak desk, finely crafted and finished, which stood at its center. No token desk was this, either, Cynthia noted immediately, from the looks of the large manila folders and envelopes that bulged their contents and the piles of open papers that were strewn about in a casually organized fashion.

Prying into Jonathan's affairs was the last thing in her mind as she walked toward the desk, yet she couldn't resist the temptation to gain a greater insight into this man she adored. As her eye jumped from paper to paper, she found most of their contents to relate to technical matters, business contracts, and similar impersonal data. One folder, however, tucked behind the others, caught her eye. Its corner extended beyond the others, enabling Cynthia to see the lettering—DRUG ENF—before the remaining letters fell behind. Curiosity getting the better of her, she gently lifted the other papers to read the rest of the writing. DRUG ENFORCEMENT ADMINISTRATION. The DEA . . . so there was a link there, she concluded, feeling a growing excitement at finding a key to some of the mystery.

Her excitement was squelched, however, when her eyes

fell to the smaller print on the front of the folder. It was with a sense of dread that she read: re Suzanne DeCarlo.

As though dropping a hot potato, she let fall the other papers to cover this disturbing bit of information. What could it mean? What could Suzanne have to do with the DEA? What did she really mean to Jonathan? 'My relationship with Suzanne is not what you think,' he had told her. What then, was it?

"I see you've been keeping busy," a cool voice broke into her thoughts, and Cynthia's eyes riveted to the door. There stood Jonathan, hands on his hips, legs in a wide stance, effectively blocking her escape. The yellow slicker he wore was dripping from the rain, leaving tiny pools of water in a circular pattern on the floor. Beads of moisture glistened on his hair and over his face, giving him an air of raw manhood. Dumbfounded, Cynthia stared at him, unable to tell what his mood was, and further, unable to produce any response of her own.

He moved toward her, his icy-blue stare impaling her. "Did you find what you were looking for?" he asked seriously.

How long had he been standing there, she wondered, as she tried to keep her wits about her. Swallowing hard, she stammered, "I w-wasn't looking f-for anything."

"Then what were you doing in here?" he demanded, still without anger yet intent on a response.

"I was just exploring. I've never been in this room." She was furious at herself for being so nervous before him. After all, she hadn't hurt anything. That's all she had really done . . . explored. Jonathan didn't have to know about what she'd seen.

As though reading her mind, his eyes dropped to the corner of the folder that remained only partly concealed. Strangely, he chose to ignore it, although Cynthia was sure that he must know she had seen it. To her greater surprise, his expression softened noticeably and he cocked his head

129

sideways, indicating that they should go into the other room.

"Come on . . . I've got some supper for us," he explained quietly, making the click of the door closing behind them seem thunderous by comparison.

By the next morning, Cynthia was feeling much better. Most of the soreness from the accident had eased, and her elbow, though tender to the touch, had ceased its ever-steady throbbing. It was with Jonathan's approval, if not enthusiasm, that she returned to her own cabin. To her dismay, however, the relief she had anticipated at being free of his all-seeing gaze did not materialize. Rather, she experienced a sense of loss, the settling in of a definite void where his presence had previously been. It was one more disturbing element to add to the many others that continued to torment her.

It being Saturday, Cynthia knew just what to expect from Jonathan. Nor was she disappointed. She sat before the window and watched him navigate his yacht beyond the craggy granite fingers which splayed from boulders at the northern end of Three Pines; moments later, the boat rounded the tip and disappeared from sight, headed west into Stonington. As she was held by the hypnotic ebb and flow of the surf, she recalled the events of the previous evening, when Jonathan had returned from the mainland. The conversation, though pleasant, had been basically uninformative.

"Were you in Stonington?" she had asked, for starters.

"No." He dipped a fried clam into tartar sauce and popped the succulent belly into his mouth in a most nonchalant manner.

"Then where *did* you go?" she persisted, ignoring the meal, so intent was she on getting some kind of an explanation.

"I wanted to speak with some friends," he replied, generously dumping french fries onto his place from the white cardboard take-out container.

"Did you contact the police?" She was now beginning to grow impatient with his lackadaisical attitude.

"Um-hum," he managed to nod, before taking a long swig of beer.

Cynthia's patience had exhausted itself. "Jonathan," she yelled, slamming a fist on the table in frustration. "Please talk to me—tell me what happened. First you get me all stirred up with your talk of two blue vans, then you walk out of here for the whole afternoon, and now all you can do is to stuff those God-awful clams into your mouth!" she fumed.

The eyes that met hers were full of innocence. "Don't you like the clams? I had to wait especially for them to be fresh fried." Only the faintest hint of a smirk graced his lips; his other features exuded an unbelievable sincerity. Somehow, she mused, with that expression on his face, he could have been a teen-ager teasing her mercilessly. The swath of sandy brown hair had fallen across his forehead in such a way that it drew attention to his eyes, glimmering azure pools that neither humored nor mocked but rather conveyed a smug determination.

She sighed, rolling her eyes upward in a gesture of exasperation. By the time she looked back at him, he had indeed given her his undivided attention.

"The clams are fine," she acknowledged in a barely controlled voice. "What isn't fine is my state of mind. You went out of here this afternoon in quite a rush, on business which I assume had something to do with me. Now, I'd like to know what came of it." Her brown eyes, widened in earnestness, begged him for a pertinent answer.

And he answered her as earnestly, his voice low and even, his eyes holding hers captive. "What came of it was nothing. The accidents have been duly reported, but beyond that there is little that can be done. You're just going

131

to have to be more careful." Was that a challenge she detected? Was Jonathan suggesting that she had been at fault in all three mishaps?

Cynthia's first impulse was to jump to her own defense. Indeed, she opened her mouth to deny his suggestion, only to close it moments later in the realization that he could be right. No, he was probably right, she concluded. It had to have been her own carelessness—what else could explain it? After all, who would want to hurt her and for what possible reason? As she dismissed the issue from her mind, she did so reluctantly, knowing that the nagging doubts would resurface before long.

That night, Jonathan had ushered her to bed on one of the bunks beneath the windows, then disappeared into the spare room without a word. When she awoke once during the night, she looked around for him, and, seeing no sign, realized that he would be sleeping in the other room. She wondered if that room was used often for sleeping, her mind's eye conjuring up an image of Suzanne and him asleep before the fire, as she had been the night before.

During the week that followed, Jonathan grew increasingly remote, only occasionally seeking out Cynthia's company. She resumed her work, if only to take her mind off him, though she remained ever aware of his comings and goings. He went lobstering as usual, but he also added an evening sail to his activities. Cynthia often hoped, as she watched him on the pier readying the yacht, that he would invite her along, but that eventuality never occurred. Rather, he would go out for several hours, retreating directly to his cabin upon his return.

On the infrequent times that he did stop in to see her, he was unusually sullen and preoccupied with his private affairs, checking up on her dutifully, perhaps delivering a letter to her or some supplies she had requested, but otherwise avoiding further involvement.

From Cynthia's point of view, his behavior was both upsetting and perplexing. She actually missed the sparring, missed the fun things they had done, above all missed *him*. Just as she rationalized that without his distracting presence, she would be able to accomplish more, the reverse turned out to be the case; she found it harder and harder to concentrate on anything other than the puzzlement of his behavior. It was as though she no longer existed in his life. other than in the perfunctory landlord-tenant, employer-employee relationship. She never would have admitted it to herself, but his indifference was infinitely more devastating than his attentiveness, whether the latter was passionate, abrasive, or ephemeral.

One day, when he arrived to bring her some fresh milk and eggs, she could stand it no longer. "What is it, Jonathan? Do I annoy you so much that you can't even manage a smile?" she blurted out, after he had placed the shopping bag on the table and turned to leave.

His head shot up and tired eyes looked at her as though only then realizing that she was there. Cynthia was taken aback by the exhaustion written over his face; for the first time his blue eyes held none of the sparkle that had always animated them.

Slowly, a wan smile molded his lips. Cynthia was startled by the look of sadness that came across in that brief moment, and her heart ached to ease it. He looked out toward the ocean, then back at her, an unfamiliar air of indecision hovering about his tall frame. Then suddenly, he seemed to gain strength.

Powerful hands drew her gently toward him, then locked behind as he hugged her. She closed her eyes; this was all that mattered to her. No words were needed. She put her arms around his waist and returned his embrace, finding strength in his muscularity and reassurance in his strength.

There was neither kiss nor caress, just a precious minute

133

of mutual comfort. She shared the tremor that passed from his body, drank in and emitted the same warmth of silent understanding, and spoke of her caring through her arms, holding tightly to him. She could have stayed that way forever, wrapped in his arms, enwrapping him in hers; all too soon, he released his hold and eased back from her.

His gaze touched her face tenderly, with a feeling she had thought to be dead and buried, if it had ever, in fact, lived in the first place.

"I can always manage a smile for you," he murmured softly, then, looking into her eyes, his brows drew together, as the mask of tension lowered once again. "You'll have to forgive me. Things . . . have been difficult this week . . . business matters . . ." The sullenness returned with a vengeance as he stalked away toward the open door.

"Isn't there anything I can do?" Cynthia yelled after him, as he started down the path. She stood in the doorway, eager to follow but fearful of his reaction should she dare.

Abruptly he stopped, turning to throw upon her the darkest, most ominous glare she had ever received. He spoke, deeply, vehemently. "Yes, Cynthia, there is something you can do. You can keep to yourself and mind your own business."

There was no way he could have missed the feeling of hurt that her features reflected in the wake of his words. If he regretted the sting, he didn't show it, though; as abruptly as he had stopped, he resumed his movement along the path toward his cabin.

The hurt and confusion continued to haunt Cynthia in the days that followed this episode. There appeared to be two distinct sides of Jonathan, at least as far as she was concerned. On the one hand, he was the compellingly strong, overwhelmingly compassionate suitor who charmed and enthralled her; on the other, he was the brash dictator, indifferent to her feelings, solely concerned with the predominance of his own. The one factor that remained constant, Cynthia rued, was his breathtaking masculinity, equally as potent and magnetic when he was for her as when he was against her.

It was a trying situation for Cynthia to face, day in and day out. There were times when she could successfully put it to the back of her mind. More often, though, she was subject to long periods of brooding that left her angry, frustrated, and desolate.

It was during one of those latter instances when, pounding furiously at her typewriter, its keys bearing the brunt of her anger, she heard a forceful knock on the door. Startled, she looked at her watch—three-thirty. Would Jonathan be back this early?

"Open up, Cynthia," the familiar voice growled. "I haven't got all day."

He wore gray slacks and a white cotton shirt, and, with the exception of the five-o'clock shadow which Cynthia had grown to adore for its roguish quality, was neatly groomed, indicating that he had not been out lobstering, as she had supposed. His eyes raked her length, as she stood at the open door in her white shorts and T-shirt, and she felt the color rise at her neck. Damn it, she thought, must he always do that to me?

"These are for you," he explained his presence bluntly, shoving two letters toward her. "One is from your uncle, the other is from a Professor G. Wittson. Who the hell is that?" His tone demanded an answer, but Cynthia ignored it in her rising fury.

She returned his stare insolently, grabbing the letters, then pulling herself up to her full five-foot, seven-inch barefooted height. "You're worse than the old-fashioned telephone operator who listens in on every conversation.

135

Would you like me to read my mail to you . . . or have you already done that?"

Jonathan was unperturbed by her insinuation, merely repeating his question, "Who is Professor G. Wittson?"

Astounded by his audacity and frazzled by her own day's torment, Cynthia exploded. "That's none of your business! I keep out of your affairs, now you keep out of mine!" If he recognized his own words within hers, he gave no indication to that effect, as he stepped forward and took her harshly by the shoulders.

"Who is Professor G. Wittson?" he demanded a final time, his voice now menacing and his powerful hands about to shake her. Cynthia knew that he would not leave without an answer.

Defiantly she stared him down. "His name is Geoffrey Wittson. He is a colleague, a fellow professor, a very good friend . . . and a gentlemanly date, I might add." Immediately, she regretted the spiteful addition, but the words had already hit their mark.

With a final, threatening stare, he released her shoulders so forcefully that she staggered back against the door jamb. By the time she regained her stance, Jonathan was well on his way. Quickly she reentered the cabin and slammed the door in belated protest of his rudeness. It was several moments before she had steadied herself enough to remember the letters in her hand.

Geoffrey's letter had been posted from Philadelphia immediately after his return from Vermont. To her envy, he had made significant headway on his book while having been in Vermont and, he wrote, although he was sorry she had not been able to join him, it did give him four totally undisturbed weeks. He hoped she was well, his letter continued, and having as much luck with her own work as he had.

"That's a joke," Cynthia muttered aloud, particularly chagrined at the latest turn her summer on Shangri-la had taken. It was her uncle's letter, formal and neatly typed under his legal letterhead, that gave her the much needed respite from self-pity. It was dated on Monday, two days earlier.

Dear Cynthia,

I hope you will forgive me from interrupting your work, but I have taken the liberty of setting up an appointment for you on this Friday morning, here in Philadelphia, with a man who could provide you with valuable inside information on organized crime as it relates to your thesis material.

Enclosed you will find a plane ticket to Philadelphia from Portland. I'm sure Mr. Roaman can help you connect. I've gone through delicate negotiations to line up this fellow, so make every effort to be here, at my office, at 9:00 Friday morning. I look forward to seeing you then, and spending a few days with you.

Your devoted uncle,
William

Thus, Cynthia found herself, two days later, in her uncle's office, deep in conversation with an organized crime courier, who was risking his life by turning state's evidence and whom William Thorpe had been hired by the state to represent. It had indeed taken some argument on Uncle William's part to convince the Attorney General to let Cynthia have some time with him, but Cynthia, although she would never let on to her uncle, was frankly disappointed in what he had to tell her. Granted, it was interesting enough to talk face-to-face with a drug mule, but she had already incorporated similar information in her dissertation from other sources, and she was surprised at her uncle's failure to recognize that, before dragging her all the way from the island.

Not that she had left against her will. She knew that she could well use a break from the oppressiveness of the recent mood on the island. It was, ironically, her very love for Jonathan that made his sullenness so devastating to her. Perhaps she would be able to put things into perspective if she got away from a bit.

Jonathan had willingly taken her by yacht to Portland, where they had taken a cab to the airport and he dutifully accompanied her onto the plane. He had been perfectly and impersonally behaved, neither too warm nor too cool, until the moment when, having seen her comfortably settled, he prepared to leave the plane.

To Cynthia's shock and puzzlement, he had glanced briefly around the half-filled plane, seated himself on the edge of the empty seat beside hers, and turned to her, taking her slender hands in his powerful ones, his strong features mere inches from her startled ones. When he spoke, his words carried a warmth that she had almost forgotten.

"I'll miss you, Cynthia." He smiled, his blue eyes sparkling through to her, drawing goose bumps up on her skin. At that moment, she forgot all of the ill feeling that had existed, be it real or imagined, during the last few days. His velvet smooth voice crooned on.

"I think you should stay in Philadelphia for a good week," he began, and, feeling her tense at his suggestion, he went on quickly, "then, I want you back with me on Three Pines. Agreed?"

Before she could react, either affirmatively or negatively, his lips claimed hers, coaxing them gently, tenderly into response, sowing the seeds of passion that could sprout and grow in seconds, given the chance, as it had been on several past occasions. It was not to be given this time, though, as he released both her lips and her hands and arose, walking quickly to the door and down the flight steps.

The memories of Jonathan stayed with her during her week at home. Her uncle had insisted that she stay at his townhouse, because she had sublet her own apartment for the summer, and, with his housekeeper in attendance, there was really very little for Cynthia to do.

She had conscientiously taken notes during her Friday morning interview with the courier, but had felt no further necessity to talk with him after that. Thus, she filled her days visiting friends, doing a smattering of work at the college library, shopping, and dining with her uncle. Had she not been preoccupied with Jonathan, it would have been a lovely break from her oftentimes futile dissertation preparation.

Quite by accident, she bumped into Geoffrey one afternoon at the library, and he promptly invited her out to dinner, a diversion she readily accepted. To her dismay, the evening had but one earth-shattering outcome: Geoffrey Wittson, at his most pleasant, interesting, intellectual, gentlemanly, and attentive, could not hold a candle to Jonathan Roaman.

It was late at night after this dinner date, with Cynthia firmly ensconced in the wing chair in her uncle's library, that Uncle William, himself, voiced what lay so heavily on her mind.

"You have fallen in love, haven't you, Cynthia?" he asked from his desk, where she had mistakenly assumed him to be engrossed in his own work.

She looked up in amazement, initially misinterpreting his implication. "With Geoffrey?" She laughed. "Certainly not!" She looked down at her hands, playing with the folds of her long terry robe. It was with utter astonishment that she heard her uncle's clarification. He had risen to join her, seating himself in the matching chair that stood opposite hers.

"You know that is not whom I mean, Cindy," he chided good-naturedly, a mischievous twinkle in his eye. "You are in love with Jonathan Roaman, are you not?"

Slowly she raised sad eyes to meet his. "You know me well, Uncle William," she said softly.

"Tell me about it," he coaxed and she readily complied, relieved to be able to share her feelings, the hopes and doubts, the fears and promises that had become her constant companions during the last weeks. Several hours later, when she finally finished spilling her thoughts to these patiently understanding ears, she paused to hear her uncle's verdict.

"I think, Cindy, that you should stay here for a few more days, and then I will see you off to return to the island. Stick with him, Cindy. Don't give up. Be patient, but stick with him." Cynthia was to recall these words many times, for they echoed the ones that Jonathan himself had used one day many weeks ago, when he had gently and caringly held her in his arms.

CHAPTER EIGHT

But now it was Suzanne whom he held in his arms, right before her very eyes! Moments earlier, Cynthia had stepped out of a taxi, intent on catching the mail boat to Three Pines. After all, it was Monday morning and there would be the regular mail delivery . . .

Monday morning . . . what was Suzanne doing here on a Monday morning? She had always arrived on Saturday and left on Sunday. Why any change now? Suddenly reality hit her almost as hard as the blue van had, at nearly this same spot, several weeks ago. Cynthia had been gone for ten days; during her absence, things must have heated up between Jonathan and Suzanne, such that she was now spending more time with him on the island.

Cynthia had been anxiously looking forward to seeing Jonathan again, to looking into those magnificent blue eyes of his, and to being held against his deliciously warm body. Now, in that instant of realization, her dream was shattered. With every bit of hope and enthusiasm draining out of her, she watched as Jonathan kissed Suzanne one last time, before helping her into her car and watching her drive off. Only then did he see Cynthia, standing forlornly at the head of the pier.

She thought she saw his face light up with some emotion, though whether it was one of surprise, pleasure, chagrin, or fury she was too far from him to decipher. Whatever it had been was quickly erased by the mask of nonchalance that replaced it. Cynthia steeled herself to his penetrating gaze as he strode toward her casually.

His eyes dazzled her as always, though his face revealed nothing more. "Hi," he drawled. "All set to go?" Without awaiting her response, he lifted her bags and headed for the yacht, which was moored further down the pier. Cynthia had no choice but to follow him.

He stowed her gear quickly and turned to see that she was indeed aboard, before he climbed on deck once again and released the lines which had secured the boat. He gave full attention to his navigation until they had cleared the harbor and were in open water, headed unusually slowly but nonetheless directly for Three Pines. Only then did he turn to Cynthia, who had been standing all the while, mutely gazing out at the ocean, the soothing ocean, strangely unable to soothe her now.

"Cynthia?" Jonathan's deep voice intruded upon the air of depression that shrouded her. Exercising every last bit of control she possessed, she stayed where she was, ignoring his bid for her attention.

As he neared her, she felt his hands, large and strong, take her shoulders and turn her to him. Cynthia could not let herself look at him, for fear of revealing the hurt and humiliation she felt. Rather, and most mistakenly, she trained her eyes lower, on the breadth of his chest, nattily clad in white oxford cloth, but open at the neck, tantalizing her with the sight of golden-brown wisps of hair which had thus made their escape.

Jonathan waited patiently for her to come to grips with her own warring senses, then could wait no longer. "Look

142

at me, Cynthia. Please." Somehow the last addition affected her and she raised her eyes hesitantly to meet his. Her composure nearly crumbled completely upon seeing his face, that beloved face, returning her gaze with something akin to . . . no, she knew it not to be. Then she heard his words, spoken soft and gently, his breath fanning over her with opiate force.

"Oh, Cyn, I've missed you so!" he whispered, as he clasped her to him with a strength that tore into her, mind and body.

It was only his shortening of her name, and the pun implied intentionally or unintentionally, which gave her the strength to resist his embrace. He felt her stiffen and slowly dropped his own arms and stood back from her.

"What's the matter, Cynthia? What's happened?" His luminous blue eyes scanned her face with such tenderness that she could only fume at his acting skill.

Not having uttered a word yet, Cynthia knew she had to say something. Taking a deep breath, she spoke through clenched teeth. "Perhaps you could tell me that."

"What do you mean?" he asked, the furrows that once she had longed to erase now appearing over his brow, this time evoking no such sympathy. Rather, a raw fury overtook Cynthia at his feigned innocence. With her fists tightly balled at her sides, she yelled at him.

"How can you do this to me, Jonathan? I saw you . . . just now . . . kissing Suzanne as lovingly as you would kiss me! How do you manage it? You really should be on the stage, you know!" she snapped bitterly. Tears of anger gathered at her eyelids and she stormed to the opposite side of the cockpit to avoid his scrutiny.

"You don't know what you saw," he began in an even voice, but he was interrupted by Cynthia's uneven one as she whirled toward him, tears running down her cheeks.

"I'm tired of hearing that—I knew exactly what I saw. I'm neither blind nor ignorant. Maybe a fool, for what

I've let happen to myself this summer . . . but not ignorant! How can you be so monstrous as to play with people's emotions like this?" She paused, struck by the puzzled look on Jonathan's face.

Quietly, he asked, his eyes glued to hers, "What *did* you let happen to you this summer?"

Amidst her anger, Cynthia marveled at how this man could always pick up on the most essential of her thoughts. Now, she had to cover for herself. "That's n-none of your business. I just want you to know that I'm conceding defeat."

"What are you talking about?"

"You didn't want a woman, or should I say, *me*, around from the very start, did you? I should have been smart enough to return on the mail boat that very first day. But I had no idea how ruthless and hateful one man could be. Well, you have tormented me one last time. You win. When we get back to the island, I'm packing and leaving here for good. At least I may be able to salvage a few weeks out of this disastrous summer!" She spat added venom into these last words, as exaggerated as she knew them to be. The thought of leaving had not occurred to her until that very moment, yet she knew instinctively that it was her wisest step. Despite both her uncle's and Jonathan's own words, she could remain near him no longer. Her fragile ego, when it came to Jonathan, could not withstand the steady battering of highs and lows of life on Three Pines. Perhaps it could have been a Shangri-la under other circumstances; for her it had become the doldrums.

Jonathan's response was low and firm. "You can't leave now. We have an agreement. You have a job to do. I have your rent money . . ."

"I don't give a damn," she shrieked back. "You keep my rent money, since you seem to need it more than I do. And as for your job, you can take it and—"

She never had a chance to finish her thought, for Jonathan began to shake her violently, stilling all words. When he finally stopped, she was ashen faced, and so weakened that she would have fallen to the floor had not his powerful arms dropped her into a nearby chair, then forced her head forward, between her knees, to restore her equilibrium. She remained thus, resting her head on her knees, while Jonathan turned his attention to the yacht. Immediately the motor jumped into high gear, speeding up dangerously as the yacht lunged ahead through the surging waves, whitecapped as ever under the stiff breeze. It was a perfect day for a sail, although neither of these potential sailors were of an appropriate temperament to consider it.

Jonathan slowed the boat only when they neared the dock at Three Pines. Crossly, he slammed the controls around, killing the motor, and charged onto the deck to secure the ropes. Cynthia took her things and made to follow him, halted suddenly by his towering figure looming in the doorway, blocking her exit. Now it was he who seethed with fury, as he glared at her menacingly.

"Was it Wittson?" he growled between thin-drawn lips.

"What?" she retorted incredulously, intimidated nonetheless by the way he stood before her, his muscular arms bracing himself on either side of the narrow doorway, making him appear even larger and more powerful than she knew, from earlier moments, him to be.

"Wittson . . ." he fumed, "Did you see Wittson in Philadelphia?"

Smarting from her own hurt and anxious to lash out in retaliation, she raised her chin in a gesture of defiance and spoke clearly. "Yes, I went out with Geoffrey while I was home." After all, she reasoned, there was no need to tell him how disastrous that date had been in her own mind, or that she doubted she would ever date Geoffrey again. All she wanted was to give Jonathan a taste of his own medicine.

The force of his stare impaled her, as it persisted. "And was it productive?" he snarled angrily.

"It certainly was," Cynthia responded, with a touch of levity in her voice designed to mislead him even more. Oh, yes, the date had been productive, but in a way totally opposite than Jonathan would imagine.

Cynthia had won this round. Deliberately, Jonathan stepped into the cabin and out of her way, gesturing that she was free to exit, which she did as quickly as she dared, not stopping once until she had reached the relative safety (was anything truly safe from men like Jonathan, she asked herself bitterly) of her cottage and had locked the door behind her, breathing a sigh of relief that he had not followed her.

As it happened, she had no worry on that score. Jonathan did not follow her then, nor was she to see him until much later that night. This fact proved to be very lucky for Cynthia, for the instant she was sure she would be undisturbed, she broke down into spasms of sobbing, which raked her body intermittently for the rest of the morning. Her tears were of anger—at Jonathan, at herself, at her uncle, and at the whole world. Her tears were of remorse—at the way she had spoken to Jonathan, at her lack of honesty, at her mishandling, in her judgment, of the entire situation. Her tears were of humiliation at having allowed herself to wind up the summer in this predicament. But, most painfully, her tears were of love, the strength of which awed her and the futility of which ravaged her.

By the time the tears had all been spent, she was thoroughly exhausted. Yet, she knew what she must do before she could hope to recover from this personal devastation. Desolately, she packed all of her things into their suitcases, as they had been when she first arrived on the island an emotional eon ago. She checked and double-checked, cleaning as she went, determined to leave the cottage as spotless as it had been on that fateful day when she had first fallen under its charm.

Then, with her heart in her mouth, she made her way the short distance up the hillside to Jonathan's cabin. It took several long moments of knocking to get a response. When the door finally opened, Cynthia found herself looking into a strangely anguished face, its blue eyes icy cold as they looked through her. He merely stared at her, as she puzzled over the pained look that dominated his handsome features. The look was so foreign to him, increasing her own pain tenfold.

She finally forced herself to speak. "Ah . . . ah . . . I need a ride to Stonington," she began weakly. "Can you give me a lift before it gets dark? I'd like to start driving tonight—"

"No!" he boomed, startling her. "I'm not going tonight. You'll just have to wait until morning."

"Then . . . maybe the mail boat . . ." she thought aloud, increasingly intimidated by his stare.

"It's too late. You'll have to wait!" She half expected the door to be slammed in her face, and was surprised that he continued to stand there, awaiting a decision that he had, indeed, already made for her.

At a loss for any smart retort, Cynthia merely turned and retraced her steps to the cabin, where she retreated to one of the sofas beneath the glass panels, and gazed out at the sea. Once again and for the last time, she thought disconcertedly, the sunset had scattered its speckles over the waves, whitecaps mingling with reds and golds in a brilliant display of nature's artistry. How many times, she mused, had she sat and witnessed this spectacle? The memory of its beauty would stay with her always, she vowed with a conviction she was surprised she still possessed.

Before her eyes, as she sat there, the warm colors of the setting sun faded into the cool blues of dusk. It was late, yet she had desire for neither food, drink, nor sleep. Her only wish was to partake, for this final time, of the wealth of the island, so pure and strong and everlasting.

The moon had risen high above the three pines before she ventured to leave her post. Perhaps, she hoped, a walk along the beach could soothe her and, even better, begin the healing process which she sensed was going to be long and painful.

It was one of the rare summer nights when the island air maintained its daytime warmth, and she had need of neither sweater nor jacket as she set out. She carried no torch; only the light of the moon, shimmering between the leafy wisps of foliage, guided her down the hillside and onto the velvet stretch of sand.

Her decision to leave the cabin was well rewarded; the beach was, indeed, a beautiful sight to behold, the moon's reflection casting long streaks of white light through the waves, which in turn beat relentlessly on the sand by her feet. It was high tide. Cynthia removed her sandals and sat down on the dry sand just above the high-water mark. She couldn't help but relax, as the soft sand molded to her shape and the cool water lapped at her toes.

She felt, more than heard, his presence. Looking up, Cynthia saw Jonathan outlined in the moonlight but a few yards from her. Involuntarily she caught her breath, as she took in his broad chest, bare and gleaming, his well-muscled arms and legs, his rugged profile as the moon drew its silhouette. He wore only denim cut-offs, and stood on the sand, muscular legs planted solidly, as though he owned it. But then, she smiled wryly, he did! Suddenly angry at the visceral response his presence evoked in her, she looked away from him.

"I have to talk to you, Cynthia," a gruff voice, which she barely recognized, spoke from a mouth she most definitely did.

Still, she refused to look at him. "There's really nothing

to say," she stated, trying to retain a coolness in her tone which belied her inner upheavals.

"I think there is," he went on determinedly. "Can I join you?"

Cynthia let out a bitter chuckle. "It's your sand."

He eased his lean frame down several feet from her and followed her gaze out over the ebbing waves. Slowly, gathering his thoughts along the way, he began. "I want you to leave tomorrow . . . but I'd like you back before Labor Day."

She turned to him in amazement. "What? You have to be kidding! No. I'm leaving tomorrow—for good!" Her voice broke on the last word and she looked down at the sand quickly, praying that he hadn't caught her anguish at the prospect of leaving.

"Why?" He was staring at her now, tearing at her resolve to maintain indifference.

"I just have to," she whispered, not looking at him.

"Is it Wittson?" he barked, anger rising abruptly.

She evaded the direct question. "Why do you torment me, Jonathan? Couldn't you have left me alone? You've got Suzanne . . . shouldn't that be enough for you?" Now she did look at him, the pleading in her eyes unmistakable in the bright light of the moon.

"Is it Wittson?" he repeated, in the same imperious tone, as though he had not even heard her words.

"Tell me, Cynthia. I have to know." Was that a hint of pleading mixed in with all the anger in his own voice, she wondered. But her frayed nerves had gone beyond understanding, and she stood up stiffly to face him.

"I said that it's none of your business. And this conversation is getting repetitive. If you'll excuse me . . ." Swiftly she turned and, in a half run, difficult as it was in the loose dry sand, headed for the hillside. She hadn't gone more than a few yards when she was tackled from behind, powerful hands on her arms pulling her down, even more powerful legs straddling her as they had done once before, pinning her on her back in the sand. Indeed, she was as hopelessly trapped as the lobsters he pulled each day.

"Do you love this Wittson?" he growled, and she knew she had to give him an answer. Unable to speak, she merely shook her head in denial of his suggestion. She couldn't lie to him; to her surprise and consternation, she didn't want to. If this was to be the last night she'd see him, she wanted him to know the truth.

Eyes brimming with unshed tears, she looked up at his face. But his attention was on her hands. Slowly, he took them into his own and brought them to his lips, kissing, ever so gently, each palm. Then he turned his gaze onto her eyes, which were open wide, rounded in confusion.

"I love you, Cyn." He spoke so softly, that she doubted she had heard him correctly. Gaining courage, he repeated his words more emphatically. "I love you, Cynthia."

Cynthia would never have believed him, had it not been for the look on his face at that moment, a look that she now knew she had misinterpreted time and time again over the course of the summer. It was unmistakable, radiating from his shimmering blue orbs, his sensuous lips, his reassuring hands. It was love, pure and simple.

Suddenly, the tears that had stood on the brink overflowed, and from deep within, Cynthia found the strength to raise her shoulders from the sand. As Jonathan simultaneously slid off her legs, she threw her arms around his neck and was crushed within the steel bands of his, her face buried in his neck, its heady scent of manliness intoxicating her. They knelt thus, on the sand, clinging to each other as they fought their way through a nightmare of misunderstandings, ill-spoken words, and lost opportunities.

Cynthia wept freely as she held onto him, aware of nothing but the hand which steadily stroked her silky smooth hair, the powerful limbs which shuddered in reaction to her body, the heart which beat furiously in rhythm with hers.

Slowly, Jonathan drew his head back and studied her tearstained features, from the fluid chocolate of her eyes to the soft fullness of her moist lips. "I love you, Cynthia," he crooned, his words caressingly tender.

For Cynthia, it was the moment of reckoning, that instant for which life itself had been destined. "And I love you, Jonathan," she whispered breathily, her deepest essence baring itself forever. "Oh, how I love you," she murmured, as the tears trickled anew over her lids.

This time, Jonathan's lips absorbed them, as his kisses covered her deep-set eyes and her delicately flushed cheeks. When he drew back again, it was for a brief moment. Emblazoned with emotion, his flickering blue eyes caressed her lips, now parted in anxious anticipation of his kiss.

Masterfully, he lowered his head and his lips captured hers, exploring their fullness, tasting their sweetness, commanding their active participation. Cynthia was willingly drawn into the fiery vortex of his passion, as his lips lowered to tantalize the sensitive lines of her neck, the hollow of her throat, the curves of her shoulders.

Her hands wound ecstatically through his lush hair, combing their way down to his neck and bare shoulders, where they reveled in each bulging sinew and every inch of firm and manly flesh.

The need of each other was mutual, as Jonathan eased her down onto her back, freeing his hands to a greater exploration of her body. His strong fingers traced the rise of her breast, their probing of its ultimate peak a sweet torture for Cynthia. She moaned aloud as his other hand skimmed her abdomen and caressed her thigh, which trembled all the more in response.

Nor was Jonathan immune to this delicious pain, as her hands roamed freely over his chest, so warm and strong and naked. They felt the span of his slim waist, the tautness of his hips, thrilling in these totally masculine contours. She rejoiced at the tremors of excitement that shot through him at her very touch. Never before had she been swept up by this joy of pleasing; never before had she known the raw pleasure of giving pleasure.

Just as the red-hot flame of passion threatened to incinerate all remaining shreds of reason, Jonathan sat up, taking Cynthia's hands into his, putting a reluctant end to her ardent wanderings. Gently, he drew her to a sitting position opposite him, holding her hands tightly as his breathing evened itself.

"*Do* you love me, Cyn?" he asked timidly, touching Cynthia's heart at its core. She wanted only to fling herself into his arms again, that being a refuge of blissful stupor. But she knew instinctively that there were explanations to be made, and she sensed that Jonathan agreed. It was a time for truth; nothing less would do to sanctify the love which had just been professed.

"Oh, Jonathan, I've loved you for weeks and weeks," she smiled shyly, marveling in hindsight that she had been able to contain the strength of it for so long.

His response was soft, with a touch of the same shyness which she felt. "I didn't know . . . so often you seemed to be put off by my approaches." He, too, felt the wasted weeks, lost now forever.

Cynthia's questioning gaze touched his. "But how could you care? You had Suzanne—" she blurted out impulsively, only to be quieted by a finger on her lips.

"I have a lot of explaining to do. But first, I need to know you love me now as much as I have loved you ever since that first day I saw you standing so bright and so very beautiful on the pier." His eyes held all the love Cynthia had ever wanted, and she responded in like form, the time for kisses having passed.

"Oh, Jonathan, if you only knew the hell I've been

152

through this summer. Wanting you . . . needing you . . . not having any idea of how to cope with my love for you. I've never been in love before . . ." She looked down at her hands as she gained control of the emotion that had crept to dangerous levels in her voice. "Do you really want to know how much I love you?" she asked rhetorically. "All summer I have been agonizing over the same questions, pushing myself and you for the answers. Now, somehow, they don't matter. No explanations are needed, as long as I know you love me!" Swiftly, he crushed her against his chest, conveying his love this time through the strength of the arms that pressed her closer to his heart.

When he finally set her back again, he shook his head. "I need to tell you. You need to know . . . if you are to know me as thoroughly as I want you to. Contrary to popular belief, love is new to me, too, Cynthia." Here, he took a deep breath and, gazing directly into her eyes, as they sat facing each other on the moon-drenched sand, the eternal pulse of Poseidon steadying them, he began his story.

CHAPTER NINE

"You see, I've spent the past few summers almost full-time here on Three Pines. Several months ago, I was approached by John Cummings—I believe you are familiar with his name—to assist in an undercover operation to nab pot smugglers along the Maine coast. Operation Lobster Trap, they call it." Jonathan smiled, half at the name and half at the look of astonishment on Cynthia's face as his story unfolded.

"Do you remember our discussion that day at lunch in Bar Harbor?" he asked gently. As she nodded, he continued. "My island is a perfect haven for this type of operation. The way the DEA figured it, with the proper plants, we could let it be known to the drug runners that I was available to work with them. My yacht would be a perfect means of transporting pot from the mother ship to the mainland, with the option of stopping midway at Three Pines, if necessary."

"But how were you to make contact with the smugglers?" Cynthia interrupted, fascinated by the intricacy of the setup.

Jonathan grinned. "You nearly blew it for me, there. You were immediately suspicious of him . . ."

Her mouth opened in amazement. "Dick?"

He nodded smugly. "That's right! Dick Young has been suspected of being a land contact for quite some time. Although he is a damned good lobsterman, there is, as you sensed, a murky side of him."

Cynthia giggled. "You can say that again." Then she sobered once again. "But what about my 'job'—why did you want a 'housesitter'?"

A tawny eyebrow arched in feigned resignation. "On that score, also, you complicated matters. You see, Cummings thought it would be a good idea to have someone around to keep an eye on things, possibly to help establish contact, certainly to act as a kind of answering service on Three Pines once contact was made. Then you showed up . . . I could no more send you away than I could draw you into the middle of all this." He sighed, kissing her fingers gently. "It seems you were drawn in anyway."

"What do you mean?" Cynthia asked hesitantly.

"None of your accidents were accidents, Cyn . . . not a one! Each of those three incidents was well planned by the smugglers' land crew. They were worried you would see too much from Three Pines. The blue van—it belongs to a fellow from Augusta, a bosom buddy of none other than our Dick!"

"I can't believe it!" she whispered, shaking her head slowly. "But the sunburn . . . surely that—"

Jonathan smiled understandingly. "That had me stumped. Every time I went swimming I tried to figure out what had banged into you, or vice versa. I scoured the bottom over and over again. Finally, about a week before you left to go back home, I found what I was looking for."

"And . . . ?" she cried impatiently.

"You were drugged, honey. Very simply. I found the

spent syringe. It was only meant to be a warning, I believe
. . . but you don't take hints very easily, do you?" He
grinned so endearingly that she couldn't help but join him.

"This whole thing is phenomenal!" Cynthia exclaimed,
as she attempted to comprehend the grand scheme.

"Wait . . . there's more!" Jonathan cautioned, rubbing
his thumbs lovingly over her knuckles. "After you'd been
hit the second time by the van and after I'd found the discarded syringe, I knew that I couldn't continue to be so
selfish as to risk your life by keeping you here. Yet I
knew—or guessed—that if I suggested you leave, you
would only be more determined to stay—"

"Uncle William!" she interrupted. "Did you really rig
that whole trip up with my uncle?" she chided.

"It was the only way I could think of to get you out of
here and under safe supervision while the buy took place
. . . that was when it really could get hot," he explained.

Now Cynthia thought aloud. "Funny . . . I sensed there
was something fishy about Uncle William insisting on my
meeting that courier . . . he knew I had that same information already." She turned her attention to Jonathan.
"Has my uncle been involved in this operation all along?"

Jonathan shook his head emphatically. "No! The fellows
from the DEA figured we had to enlist his aid for this one
matter, but he knew nothing of it prior to then. I talked
with him on the phone several times last week . . . he
sounds like a terrific guy!"

"That he is," she confirmed, as her mind continued its
frantic sorting-out process. "But Jonathan, why couldn't
you tell me sooner? Why now?"

"We had to assume that the more you knew the greater
a threat you would be to these thugs. It looks like they
feared you anyway."

Suddenly things fell into place enough for Cynthia to
remember something he had said moments earlier. "The
buy," she cried, "did it go off as planned?"

For the first time in his story, Jonathan frowned and worry lines reappeared on his forehead. "Unfortunately not," he replied quietly. "Would you believe that we were fogged in for most of last week?"

Cynthia's eyes opened wide in understanding. "Then, has it been rearranged?"

Slowly, he nodded. "If the weather holds, Dick and I will be going out the day after tomorrow. I'll be wired up with all kinds of electronic equipment, as is the yacht. The people from the DEA want to follow through with the entire operation, nabbing not only the mother ship—if we can lure it inside the twelve-mile limit—but the on-shore couriers as well. They have assured me that if Dick agrees to testify for the state, he will be granted immunity from prosecution."

A sudden pall had befallen them, as the reality of the danger to be faced hit home. For Cynthia, however, the pall had an added dimension. As her mind assimilated all that Jonathan had told her, she realized that there was only one outstanding piece to the puzzle, the major one, without which the power of the love which Jonathan claimed to hold for her would be rendered impotent.

Adept at reading her thoughts, Jonathan smiled broadly, his even teeth reflecting the white of the moonlit beach. "Out with it, love . . . ," he teased.

The prospect of what she had to ask pained her terribly. Suddenly unsure, both of Jonathan and of her own ability to live with the explanation he might give, she faltered, seeking courage from the strength of the waves that crashed against the rocks further down the beach.

It was Jonathan who spoke first, voicing the name that Cynthia could not. "Would you like to know about Suzanne?" he asked gently, his tone of tender understanding melting her insides. The most she could manage was a nod, as she searched his eyes for what was to come.

A smile broke over Jonathan's features, suggesting that

he intended to enjoy this pièce de resistance. "For starters," he began, "Suzanne DeCarlo is not my secretary." Cynthia's blood froze in dread, suddenly reluctant to hear that which she had suspected all along. Before she could halt his words, Jonathan continued, firmly and with conviction. "Nor is she, or was she ever, my lover." Something immediately relaxed within Cynthia, only to be stirred anew by confusion. Prompted by her expression of bewilderment, Jonathan proceeded to put the final piece into the puzzle.

"Suzanne DeCarlo is a policewoman, working out of Washington, as an undercover agent with the DEA," he explained with great satisfaction at his coup.

Cynthia struggled to keep up. "But . . . w-what did she do?"

Smugly he continued. "As you know, there are no phones on Three Pines. Suzanne has been my contact with the authorities. By posing as my girlfriend, she was able to come every weekend. However, her suitcase was filled, not with the flimsy negligees you imagined, but with letters and instructions for me from the DEA."

"B-but your act was so real . . . how could I th-think otherwise . . . and why was she here today, on a Monday?"

"To begin with, our act *had* to be good, so that no one would suspect her real motive for coming here. There had to be public shows of affection, my raving about her before Dick, and so on. At first it was easy—that is, until you arrived on the scene. Somehow, you managed to bewitch me into that awful sense of betrayal each time Suzanne and I put on our demonstration!" A mischievous twinkle in his eye was fit accompaniment for his words.

"As for why she was here on a Monday, a few changes had to be made in the overall plan when the buy was rescheduled," he explained. "Your absence gave us the

158

perfect cover to let Suzanne stay longer and better prepare me for . . ."

Cynthia had taken her hands from his and buried her face in them, her words half smothered but nonetheless audible. "Oh, Jonathan! I've been such a fool!"

Quite deliberately, he took her into his arms, and consoled her. "We've both been fools, Cyn. I thought you hated me on sight at some points, while at others I sensed the opposite. Yet how could I profess my love for you and then continue to lie to you about this operation? I've lived in torment for these last weeks, loving you and wanting you yet unable to tell you so. Even now, Cyn, Cummings assumes you are in the dark." He took a deep breath to steady himself, as he went on.

"You've got to leave the island until this is all over. I can't bear the thought of your being exposed to this risk. It's my escapade, not yours." Now he spoke with the command in his tone that she knew so well. "You'll leave tomorrow morning and go down to Portland, where it will be easier for you to get lost in the crowd. I'll call ahead from the mainland and make reservations at the Sheraton there. Then I'll call you as soon as this thing is over." He took her shoulders somberly. "It's the only way, Cyn. Don't you agree?"

"Can't I be of some help here? I'll be a nervous wreck sitting all alone down there wondering what's happening here . . ."

"No," he insisted. "I can't allow you to stay. Please don't give me a hard time, Cyn. It's going to be hard enough as it is!"

Put that way, Cynthia had no option but to agree to this. There was no way she would knowingly complicate things for him. She took a long, deep breath, inhaling the tangy salt air of the sea and the musky male scent of Jonathan, so close now in body and soul.

Giving in to her clamoring senses, she raised her hands

and tentatively touched his bare chest, delighting in the roughness of the manly tufts of hair at her fingertips. Lovingly, she stroked his shoulders and arms, before drawing her hands back to his muscle-rippled chest. Jonathan smiled at the look of wonder on her face.

"You look like a little girl who has just received her first fuzzy stuffed animal . . ."

She smiled bashfully at him. "It's so beautiful . . ." she whispered.

Jonathan groaned and pulled her roughly into his embrace. "Oh, honey, what am I going to do with you?" he growled huskily. "You've driven me half mad all summer long, and now you're determined to finish the job."

Before Cynthia could deny it, his lips had seized hers roughly, punishing them appropriately for her crime. The gentleness and teasing were gone, replaced by a heady domination, a bruising command, which stimulated her yearnings even more. She was his prisoner, thriving in her captivity. When he abruptly released her lips, they both gasped for air.

Jonathan held her in his arms and studied her features for several long minutes. "Let's go for a swim," he drawled, a devilish twinkle in his eye, the practicality of his suggestion not lost on Cynthia.

She smiled as she teased, "That would be a very wise idea . . . except for one small matter. We have no bathing suits on . . . and mine are packed at the bottom of my suitcases."

Gently, he smoothed a strand of hair from her cheek. "I don't mind . . . if you don't . . ." His deep huskiness sent tremors anew to her every nerve end. In any other situation, she would have indignantly refused such an offer. Now, however, those strange happenings had seized her body, heightening her longings to an unbearable level. And his suggestion excited her all the more.

As though in a trance, Cynthia moved back from Jona-

160

than and stood up. His eyes followed her every movement as she slowly drew her jersey up over her head, then let it fall to the sand. It was with trembling fingers that she touched the front closing of her bra, then unhooked its clasp and let it drop likewise. Shyly, she lifted her eyes to his, to find a wealth of adoration in his gaze which precluded any self-consciousness she might have felt at standing bare-breasted before him. Jonathan stood up then and reached for the zipper of his jeans as she reached for hers.

A moment later, all trappings of civilization discarded on the beach, they stood before one another, man and woman, their nakedness primitive and gleaming in the moonlight. The short space between them evaporated in an instant of mutual desire. Cynthia caught her breath in sharply as his arms closed about her and her body touched his, skin against skin, limb against limb, driving her ecstasy to a fevered pitch.

"That water better be damned cold," Jonathan swore under his breath as he swung her lithely off her feet and into his arms and effortlessly carried her into the water. She was numbed to all else but the warmth of his chest against her breast, the firmness of his abdomen against her hip, and the strength of his arms around her bare back and under her legs.

Just as the water touched her bottom, Jonathan dropped her mischievously and unceremoniously into the waves. Although caught by surprise, she quickly surfaced and retaliated in kind, splashing and kicking, dragging at his arms until he had been similarly submerged.

They romped thus, round and about, touching, separating, swimming out then back, all the while expecting the cool water to quench the flame of their smoldering passion. But it was not to be; the coolness merely drove them together, relishing all the more the warmth they could give each other. As they swam, each fought his own private war of self-control, again to no avail.

161

As they approached one another a final time, chest deep in the gentle waves, Cynthia willingly waived the long-ingrained moral code she had hitherto lived by. It was no longer valid. For, she realized then that the soundest and most basic validity in life was love. She loved Jonathan as he loved her; nothing else mattered.

It was inevitable; between the emotion and the chemistry, it was not to be denied. In an act of total commitment, Cynthia wrapped her arms around Jonathan's neck and was drawn into the web of his manhood. Her body floated against his, then arched in response to her own cravings. His hands caressed her shoulders, ran down her spine to the small of her back, massaged her legs as they wound around him.

She swam willingly into the whirlpool of passion, responding instinctively to his needs as to her own. He guided her masterfully down this new and wondrous path, the light at its end beckoning, beckoning to unimagined ecstasy. The inevitable moment of pain was borne, then forgotten, obliterated from her memory by the joy she felt to be as one with Jonathan, striving together toward the peak of fulfillment. With the waves as their magic carpet, they rose up, up, up to heights unseen, on their own very intimate, very passionate, very religious high.

There was neither guilt nor misgiving as they lay in each other's arms, much later, before the fire in Jonathan's cabin. "Sleeping?" he asked her gently, looking down at her lowered lids.

She shook her head and snuggled closer against him, resentful only of the clothes which he had insisted, for the sake of sanity, they put on. "No way! I'm not missing one minute of this!" she teased, possessively spreading an arm across his chest.

Deliberately he removed her arm and sat up, grinning at her expression of disappointment as he leaned down and

162

kissed the tip of her nose. "I have something for you . . . stay here," he ordered. He disappeared into the other room, returning moments later with one hand behind his back. Cynthia sat up questioningly.

"Close your eyes," he commanded. She obeyed. She felt his hands at the nape of her neck, securing the clasp of what had to be a necklace, she guessed, from the shape of it around her neck. When he was satisfied with his work, he gave his permission. "Okay, now you can look."

Cynthia opened her eyes and gazed with disbelief at a magnificent diamond ring that lay, suspended from a gold chain, well below the hollow of her throat. As she fingered it in astonishment, it twinkled a reflection of the crackling fire, emitting blue sparkles like those in Jonathan's eyes. At a loss for words, she turned her gaze on the latter.

"Marry me, Cyn," Jonathan commanded softly, his eyes conveying all the need and the love he felt for her, effectively turning his order into a plea. "I'll love you forever . . . without you, forever is meaningless! Will you marry me?"

She was stunned. It only then occurred to her that she had given of her love—and her body—with no thought of marriage. There had been no strings attached, save those of the love which bound them together. This was an unexpected turn of events which boggled her mind.

"W-when did you buy it?" she gasped breathlessly.

"The day you left for Philadelphia, I stayed at the airport and caught a plane to New York. I returned the next morning . . . with this." He touched the ring, himself, his fingers warm against her throat, thrilling her. Bending her head, she kissed his hand, encircling it with her own.

"I love you . . . I love you," she murmured in a daze of ecstasy.

"But will you marry me?" He brought her back to the moment.

Cynthia smiled as she looked into his eyes. "I don't have any choice, do I?" she teased.

He looked suddenly stricken. "You mean, because of last night—?"

"No, silly!" she laughed. "But I love you all the more for that! No, I have no choice but to marry you simply because I can't live without you. I realized that during my stay back in Philly. No, I realized it even earlier, when you became so distant and I didn't see you for days at a time. I've never been so miserable!" She shivered in remembrance of the nights she had cried herself to sleep.

"There will be no more torment on that score!" Jonathan vowed, taking her left hand in his. Caressing her ring finger, he explained, "The chain is only temporary. As soon as this DEA business is over, the ring goes here. But only for a day or two, until we can be married! Then it will go here." He pointed to the ring finger of her right hand, lifting it to his lips very gently. "I don't believe in long engagements," he murmured against it, looking mischievously up at her eyes.

"I wonder why . . ." she smirked. Playfully, Jonathan tackled her and pinned her down onto the cushions.

"Will you marry me, Cynthia?"

"Yes, Jonathan, I will!"

They watched the sunrise together that morning. In Cynthia's mind it was nothing short of a miracle. So much had happened to her since she had last seen the sun, so long yet mere hours ago. Was it possible for her love to have grown even stronger? Yet that was how she felt as she looked up at the ruggedly handsome face next to hers.

"Beautiful, isn't it?" Jonathan asked, as the pale yellow streaks appeared, weak at first, but steadily stronger, on the horizon.

Cynthia agreed, "Mmmm," trying to decide which was

more beautiful, the sunrise or her love for this man whose arm protectively held her against his tall frame.

It was indeed a new day they faced, created both before their eyes and within their hearts. No, thought Cynthia, the sunrise would always pale in comparison with the great adoration she felt for Jonathan. It was totally indescribable, but she would bask in it forever.

Once again, he read her thoughts, echoing them in his own words, as he gave her a breath-stopping hug. "You know, Cyn, I've seen the sunrise from just this spot dozens of times. Never has it been so beautiful as it is today." Gently, he kissed her forehead. "Perhaps, though, I'm confusing the beauty of the sunrise with your beauty . . . our beauty."

Ever so naturally, as though she had been born to be just where she was, Cynthia wound her arms around his neck and their lips met in one infinitely hallowed, gloriously beckoning kiss.

Cynthia arrived in Portland late in the day, having slept but a few hours in the morning, before Jonathan had shuttled her to Stonington. She had tried a final time to convince him to let her stay, but his mind was firmly and irrevocably set. Thus it was, with repeated assurances that he would contact her once the buy was made, and with a proper show of indifference in front of the townspeople, that Jonathan had seen her safely off in her car.

The drive, though only a matter of several hours, was tedious. Her mind and heart were back at Three Pines. That was where she wanted to be—not driving in the opposite direction! Her only consolation was the ring dangling brilliantly above her heart, a dazzling reminder of the man and the relationship that awaited her at the end of what promised to be an agonizing few days. She had brought some work with her to do, but even as she had

165

packed it in her suitcase she suspected that most of it would remain untouched.

As Jonathan had promised, the hotel was expecting her. What Cynthia hadn't been prepared for was what "expecting" meant, à la Jonathan Roaman. From the instant she had identified herself at the main desk, she was treated like nothing short of royalty. Her bags were swooped up by a burly bellhop and she was gallantly whisked off to a three-room suite, luxuriously designed and elegantly furnished.

"This is really larger than I need," she protested apologetically to the hotel manager, who had personally escorted her to the suite. As she looked around her, she wondered if she even had enough money with her to pay for such luxury. Her thoughts were cut off, however, by the manager's cheery insistence.

"Mr. Roaman's orders . . . only the best for Professor Blake!" he smiled, showing her the pertinent facilities in the suite, then quietly taking his leave.

Cynthia smiled . . . Professor Blake. Could it be that Jonathan was proud of her? Just then, her eye caught on a huge arrangement of fresh flowers in the center of the round coffee table, and it was as though she had been instantly transported back to Three Pines. Here were the wild flowers that had grown on the hillside—the pert daisy, the saucy black-eyed Susan, the dainty buttercup—artfully blended with dozens of the most delicate, most divinely aromatic baby roses she had ever seen. It was a blend of reds and whites and yellows, a mass which, through the mist of tears that had sprung to Cynthia's eyes, simulated the sunset which she so revered. It was the sunset to which she had bid farewell so sadly just last night, never dreaming that she would see it again. Now she knew that she could look forward to seeing it again and again.

It was only by accident that she caught sight of the card

that was all but buried amid the profusion of petals, stems, and leafy greenery. Excitedly she opened it, her heart thumping beneath its diamond protector.

TO MY BELOVED PROFESSOR—WHO HAS
ALREADY TAUGHT ME SO VERY MUCH!

L.J.R.

Cynthia smiled through her tears. As she inhaled the scent of the fresh-cut roses, she knew that, short of his being there himself, there could have been no other gesture more soothing. She put the card back on the table and sprawled out on the king-size bed, gazing at the flowers until weariness overtook her and her eyelids reluctantly flitted down, long brown lashes feathered high atop her cheek bones, as she fell into a sound sleep.

When she awoke several hours later, the sun had already set. Quickly she washed her hands and face, changed into a fresh sundress, touched up her makeup, and went down to the hotel restaurant for dinner. Once again, she was treated like a queen, escorted to a beautifully set table by a window overlooking the street, attended by the wine steward, who delivered a bottle of wine "compliments of Mr. Roaman," and the maitre d', who enthusiastically elaborated on the menu and made his personal recommendations, then chivalrously gave her order to the waiter, who had stood by all the while in a most solicitous manner.

This kind of treatment was something totally new for Cynthia, who, although she had eaten in many fine restaurants, had never been catered to with such zeal before. It would have been quite an experience, she thought longingly, if only Jonathan had been there to share it with her.

As impressed as she had been by the obvious respect that the name Roaman had commanded, a strange unease had begun to set in by the end of the meal. Actually, Cyn-

167

thia realized in hindsight, she had begun to sense the faint nagging even on the road earlier in the day . . . each time a blue vehicle (and heaven knows there had been plenty) had passed her. Even the wine couldn't mask the awareness that practically everyone in this hotel seemed to know who she was. Jonathan had assured her that there would be anonymity here, yet his own gestures, loving as they were, had precluded that. No, the wine certainly didn't ease the feeling that she was being watched. Or perhaps it was because of the wine that she was beginning to imagine things. Why was the murky dark-haired man staring at her?

But, of course, it was nothing, she chided herself. Men always stared at women who were alone. Quickly she looked away from him, touching the ring at her throat for reassurance as she signaled the waiter for her check.

"It's already been taken care of, miss," he informed her, then, in answer to the look of bewilderment on her face, explained, "Mr. Roaman has instructed your bills to be put on his private account."

Rigidly, Cynthia smiled and nodded, feeling all the more awkward at this unexpected turn of events. Jonathan had really taken over, hadn't he? But why was she bothered by this? Certainly not for the act, itself; actually, she would have been hard put to come up with the cash to pay for the suite and meals like this every night, and, once they were married, it would be perfectly natural for him to pick up the tab. However, they weren't married yet, and she had the faintest sense of being a temporarily "kept" woman.

What really puzzled her, more than anything else, was why he had insisted she leave Three Pines for her own safety, then had all but advertised her identity here in Portland. In an attempt to ease her skittishness, she returned directly to her suite, bolting the doors securely before she bathed and lay down with a book until sleep came.

168

To her dismay, this same nervousness returned to haunt her the next day. She had slept late, breakfasted leisurely—was that the same dark-haired man looking at her over her coffee cup, it was hard to tell—and then abandoned the thought of work on an impulse to go sightseeing . . . anything to keep her mind occupied, she vowed, little realizing that she had set for herself an impossible feat.

On the advice of the hotel's recreation director, she hesitantly joined a bus tour that was departing at that same time. Normally Cynthia avoided this type of thing, preferring to move about freely and on her own. However, a small part of her sensed that not only would there be the steady monologue of the guide to occupy her mind, but there would also be safety in numbers (how absurd, this paranoia, she reproached herself, as she nonetheless climbed aboard the bus with a score of other tourists).

Well, this is the day; I wonder when the buy is going to be made, she thought, as the tour guide launched into a dissertation on Henry Wadsworth Longfellow, whose native city Portland was. Probably tonight, in the safety of darkness, she concluded, turning her gaze on the stately elms that lined the streets.

Cynthia was in for a jolt when the bus pulled up at the Wadsworth-Longfellow House and its passengers filed out. There, several people behind her, was the same dark-haired man, tall and lean as he stood among the others, wearing a business suit and dark glasses. In her opinion, his attire and manner, so un-touristlike, set him off from the rest . . . or was it all her imagination? Was he looking at her? It was difficult to tell, with his sunglasses camouflaging his gaze. Uncomfortably, Cynthia moved forward, putting as much distance as possible between that ominous character and herself.

The group moved on, visiting the Tate House and the Victoria Mansion, charming period residences which had been restored, and in some cases contained the original

169

furnishings and artwork. I wonder whether Dick is going to be with Jonathan when the actual buy is made? What if he tries to injure Jonathan? A chill passed through her as she temporarily forgot the man who frightened her in her apprehension for Jonathan's safety.

The Portland Museum of Art was inspiring, as was the Maine Historical Society Museum. Would Suzanne be coming up for the buy? Would she be there to help should Jonathan run into trouble? Wasn't it ironic, Cynthia mused, that now she relished the idea of Suzanne being with him!

Cynthia had always admired lighthouses, and the Portland Headlight was no exception. She was particularly interested when the guide explained that it had been the first lighthouse authorized by the United States government on specific orders from General Washington, and that it was the oldest lighthouse in constant use today. If only Three Pines had a light, she wished. What if there was some mishap in the dark of night? Did Jonathan have radar on his yacht? She had never thought to ask!

As the bus stopped before an old barrel factory, the last remaining one of its kind on the waterfront, Cynthia became once again aware of the dark stranger who, but for her aroused imagination, would seem to be following her. He was paying about equal attention to the murky insides of the factory and to her, she noted with a faint shudder, unable now to miss the sidelong glances he repeatedly threw her way.

It was with a sigh of relief that she stepped off the bus back at her hotel, making a beeline for the safety of her room. Well, the tour had certainly given her something else to consider, she winced, as she dialed for room service and ordered a Coke and a salad.

Was she merely being paranoid, she asked herself, as she gazed at her reflection in the mirror. How she had changed since she had left Philadelphia last spring! Her skin now boasted an evenly tanned hue, which together with her brown features gave her an air of inner richness that she had never seen before. In addition, there was the uniquely flattering flush that dappled her cheeks, giving her a radiance for which only Jonathan could be responsible.

Then what about this lean and dark stranger . . . was he drawn to her as the attractive woman she had to admit she was . . . or was his attention more sinisterly founded? Had it not been for her three previous unfortunate incidents, she would have paid no heed to his presence. In light of them, however, she was wary. Should she call Jonathan? But there was no way to reach him. And even if there had been, he would have his own worries right about now!

Troubled thus, Cynthia spent the rest of the day going through the motions of working on her dissertation. But such concentration proved to be almost as elusive as sleep would be that night.

Early the next morning, Cynthia ventured into the coffee shop, where she proceeded to scour the newspaper for any word of the pot bust which, according to her calculations, would surely have taken place by then. Nothing! No lead story, no brief paragraph, no terse sentence . . . nothing, she concluded with disappointment as she folded the newspaper and turned her attention to the breakfast that sat, suddenly quite unappetizing, before her.

The sooner the sale was over, the sooner she would be able to rejoin Jonathan. What had happened, her thoughts screamed in frustration. Trembling fingers raised a coffee cup to her lips. Over its rim, a sight caught her eye that made her stomach lurch. There sat the brooding man, her unwanted shadow, lingering over his breakfast at a table not far from hers.

Cynthia could stand the silent torment no longer. Determinedly rising to her feet, she astounded herself by boldingly approaching this man, who, she was convinced, had calmly and most maddeningly observed her every movement since her arrival in Portland two days before.

"Do I know you?" she demanded imperiously, shocked at what the human condition could produce under such trying circumstances.

The shaded eyes studied her. "No. I don't believe so." The voice was bland and impersonal.

"Should I know you?" she persisted, with a sense of growing annoyance.

Still, he studied her. "No. I don't believe so." The same nondescript tone responded to her demand.

Nerves drawn taut, Cynthia feared that she was on the verge of some inner explosion. Speaking in a low and barely controlled voice, she threatened, "Look . . . I get the distinct feeling that you are following me. Now, if it continues, you may find yourself answering to the police. Am I making myself clear?"

Slowly, an insolent smile spread over the stranger's cold lips. "I'm sorry, miss. You must be mistaken. I'm here on business."

"Then keep to it," she snapped, turning on her heel and exiting in a huff of feigned confidence without a look behind her. It was only when she stood once more in her suite, back against the bolted door, that tremors of fear shook her. So he had claimed innocence, she marveled . . . what gall! Unless she had become totally paranoied . . .

It was for two more long and terror-filled days that Cynthia awaited some word about Operation Lobster Trap, leaving her room only for an occasional meal, having the others delivered by room service. Finally, on the fifth morning of her stay in Portland, the newspaper headlines broke the story.

In a federally coordinated effort, a freighter loaded
illegally with marijuana from Colombia, better known
as Santa Marta Gold, was seized by the Coast Guard
after undercover agents, posing as couriers, lured the
mother ship within the twelve-mile limit. In addition
to the freighter and its crew, two on-shore vans and
their drivers were arrested in what is thought to be
the largest such seizure to date. Following months of
planning and set-ups by the Drug Enforcement Administration, the FBI, and State Police, the sting operation took place last night off the coast of
Stonington . . .

Cynthia's eye skimmed the columns that detailed the operation for some mention of Jonathan's name, but there was
none. Was he all right, she wondered apprehensively.
There had been no mention of violence in the paper,
which had literally splashed the story over the first four
pages, interviewing this policeman and that automobile
mechanic and the other high school principal, all of whom
gave personal, though totally unenlightening, interpreta-
tions of the bust and its implications.

No, she rationalized, Jonathan had to be all right,
though her wildly imaginative mind conjured up images of
a deadly syringe danging from his arm as his body was
pulled from the sea, or the charred ruin of his cabin on
Three Pines, its occupant burned beyond recognition. But
then, his name had certainly been kept out of the papers
for precisely that purpose—to assure his anonymity and
thereby maximize his own safety!

All day, she sat by the telephone in her hotel room.
Room service had come to know her well, bringing the
latest newspaper editions as they arrived. She was unaware

of the limited menu offered her, so far from the thought of food was her agitated mind.

Why doesn't he call? What could be keeping him? Where is he now? Over and over again, the same questions nagged at her. Finally, a full forty-eight hours after the headlines had first appeared in the newspaper, she could stand it no more. Packing her bags with unprecedented speed, she called for her car to be brought out, and, without a word from Jonathan, she headed for Stonington.

CHAPTER TEN

What she was to encounter upon her arrival there, she was totally unprepared for. It was a rerun of one other morning, that same sense of déjà vu which had hit her once too often this summer. As her car pulled up to the pier, there was Jonathan, in the warm and slenderly exquisite arms of a beaming Suzanne.

Flabbergasted, Cynthia froze where she was, unable to think, plan, move, or understand. How could this be, she cried inwardly, as the tears welled behind her lids. In a state of shock, she could only stare ahead at the outward show of affection playing before not only her own but the eyes of the town. According to what Jonathan had said, his relationship with Suzanne had been nothing more than a cover. If so, why was he upholding it when the operation was over and done? Cynthia had sat on pins and needles in her hotel room in Portland, awaiting that phone call which had never come, when all along Jonathan had been making the most of his time with Suzanne!

Fingers frantically clasping the diamond at her throat, Cynthia groped for possible explanations, but, in her agitated state, found none. How could Jonathan have pledged

his love to her a mere week ago and given her this diamond ring as a symbol of their engagement, then resumed
his play with Suzanne? Was that how he expected their
marriage to be? If so, it was not for Cynthia!

Infuriated, she dropped the ring from her fingers,
slammed the transmission into drive, and turned the corner into the municipal parking lot which abutted the main
street. Lingering in her car just long enough to allow Jonathan and Suzanne their good-byes and departure, she
made for the pier. Having calculated corerectly, there was
sign of neither of them, as she crossed the street in front
of the Post Office. At least someone was on her side, she
noted bitterly, as she intercepted the mailman on the way
to his boat. Once aboard, the boat sputtered its way out of
the picturesque harbor and began its round-about course
which would take her, for the last time, to Three Pines.

Having caught sight of Jonathan's yacht at the pier in
Stonington, Cynthia had no fear of meeting him on her arrival at the island. With a knot of anguish gnawing at her
stomach, she stumbled up the hillside, noting that, contrary to her terror-filled imaginings, both cabins still stood,
sturdy and proud, their glassy eyes blinking a starlike reflection of the sun at her as she ran.

Halfway up the hillside she stopped, remembering in a
flash that she had neither mentioned to the mailman to
stop back for her on his round trip nor put up the red flag
that would likewise hail him. Soundly reproaching herself
for her negligence, she retraced her steps to the pier, put
the flag securely in its holster, then made her way once
more to the cabin.

There was actually very little packing to do; most of her
things were still in the suitcases as she had placed them on
that day, not long ago, that she had similarly prepared to
leave. But although her heart had been heavy on that day,
it was nothing compared with the excruciating pain that

tore through her now. This emotional seesaw had taken its toll on her; she was a ball of raw nerves wrapped in a flimsy layer of composure which had just about worn through.

Heartbroken and totally distraught, she felt she couldn't endure a moment longer on the island; but there was no alternative to waiting for the mail boat. Her only hope was that she should be spared the sight of Jonathan, knowing that the anguish of such a reunion would dissolve her fragile ego altogether.

Blinded by tear-filled eyes, she made her way to the apex of the island and her beloved three pines. Beneath their frond canopy, she sank down onto the soft cushion of pine needles that carpeted the small plateau. Deeply she inhaled the tangy fragrance of the woods, lush and green both above and below. But this time, rather than enchanting her with its natural headiness, the scent of all she loved tore even deeper into her, as though her reunion with this cherished spot had done the very damage she had feared from Jonathan.

Uncontrollably, she broke down into convulsive sobs, with neither the strength nor the desire for restraint. Tears flowed freely over her soft features, overspilling the chocolate pools of her eyes, matting her long brown eyelashes, streaking her bronzed cheeks, making their underlying pallor all the more apparent. Arms about her middle, she rocked to and fro, seeing nothing, hearing nothing. It was an outpouring of grief, the anguished mourning of a love which lived so briefly and so beautifully and then had been lost.

When the sobs had subsided, Cynthia rested her silky brown head atop the pillow of needles and lay down, all consumed by the misery that stalked her. A small voice inside her warned her to keep a lookout for the mail boat, but her limbs were unable to muster even the slightest movement in that direction. Rather, she was mesmerized by the image which recurred in painfully vivid clarity before her eyes. It was that of Jonathan's face, in all its rugged handsomeness, his white teeth gleaming through well-formed lips, his nose with its rakish set and his sandy hair appealingly windblown. But most compelling of all were those eyes she knew so well, extensions of the blue sky above, which twinkled their love at her.

Lies! Deceit! Betrayal! her mind screamed, as she bolted up in anger at the reality of the image. Then, she bolted once more at the reality of the reality. For there, clear as life before her, knelt Jonathan, a look of bewilderment having replaced the one of smug confidence which her mind had painted.

"What is it, Cynthia?" he asked, stretching out sinewy arms to take her shoulders, then withdrawing them as she shrank from his touch. "What happened, honey? Please tell me . . ." he begged earnestly. Were those tears in his eyes that she saw or merely remnants of her own?

"Don't touch me," she cried desolately. "Just go away . . ." Her voice trailed off as, predictably, she broke down before him. Quickly she turned away, crumbling in a heap under the shadow of the pines.

Firm hands grasped her shoulders and turned her to him, but she fought him, pounding her fists against him, flailing at his arms and chest as though they were the injustices, real and imagined, which assailed her, striking wildly at his face in recollection of its shows of false emotion, kicking out at the legs that had so proudly stood on the sand he owned. On the brink of hysteria, she screamed his name over and over again, punishing herself with its rhythm as she tried to punish him with her ineffectual beating.

Suddenly, the will to fight was gone, and he captured her within the circle of his arms, smothering her sobs against the solid wall of his chest, absorbing her spasms in

178

his pliant form. "Shh . . . shhh . . . it's all over, honey," he crooned against the sweat-matted line of her bangs.

"It's all over . . . it's all over," she repeated weakly, attempting to draw away from him but being held immobile against him by his powerful arms. "Let me go," she pleaded once more. "It's all over . . ."

Slowly Jonathan did loosen his grip, but only enough to draw back and see her face without giving her the opportunity to run from him. "What are you saying, Cynthia?" he asked in a sober voice.

Mustering every ounce of strength her racked body held, she faced him straight on. "I waited and waited for your call. I was so worried that something terrible had happened to you. Why didn't you call? Finally, I couldn't stand the waiting any longer, so I packed up and drove back to Stonington. I saw you, Jonathan. I saw you with Suzanne. It's not me you love . . . it's her, just as she loves you." Her lower lip quivered in its softness, her insides aching all the more at the look of sadness which had appeared on his face. Silently, he shook his head. Was he denying her accusation or merely regretting that she had seen enough to make it? Cynthia was too drained emotionally to ponder such issues. Rather, she made a final soulful plea. It was but a whisper, though Jonathan caught her every word.

"Please let me leave. Go to her. I love you too much to deny you such happiness . . ."

Suddenly Jonathan's expression changed to one of impatient anger. "Stop it, Cynthia . . . now!" he barked crossly. Then, with features softening, he spoke gently again. "It's you I love, Cyn. Not Suzanne! Don't be a fool—"

"Fool?" she screamed. "That's just what I am . . . an absolute fool for falling in—"

A solid hand clamped over her mouth, silencing her as she was pushed back onto the bed of pine needles and pinned down by a viselike arm across her chest. If she had been hysterical, his movement snapped her out of it.

"That's enough!" he commanded in that tone of authority she knew well. "Now I want you to listen to me and I don't want any interruptions," he growled. "What you saw earlier was nothing more than the fond farewell of two people who have worked closely for several months but will be doing so no longer. No longer!" he repeated, placing equal emphasis on both words.

Gently, he brushed her hair back from her tearstained cheeks, grazing her dampened eyelashes ever so lightly as he did. "I wanted to call you. In fact, that was the only thing I wanted to do. But Cummings had other ideas. He insisted on debriefings and on keeping me in total isolation until they were completed. We went over and over the same story. I finally threatened to clam up completely if he didn't let me go this morning. When I tried to reach you, you had checked out!" He paused, as though putting the past far behind.

But for Cynthia, the past was still at her shoulder. "It was so terrible in Portland . . . the waiting . . . not knowing. And that horrible man . . ."

"What man?" he interrupted, a spark flashing dangerously in his eye.

"This strange dark-haired man, always wearing a business suit and dark glasses . . . everywhere I went, there he was . . . it was so frightening!" Her fears were temporarily reborn in her eyes.

Strangely, Jonathan seemed most relieved. "Oh, honey! I'm sorry he frightened you! But he was only doing his job—"

"What?" she exclaimed incredulously.

"I finally told Cummings about you and he insisted they give you a bodyguard, especially in light of what you'd already gone through!"

Cynthia looked away from him in embarrassment. In a

barely audible voice she whispered, "I must be absolutely paranoid. I've never been like this before."

But Jonathan comforted, "You had good reason to be afraid, after what happened earlier. But that's all over now. I love you, Cynthia. And I've never been like this before!" Suddenly his eyebrows lifted in remembrance. "Here . . . I have something for you." He reached into the breast pocket of his blazer and withdrew a small white envelope and an even smaller box. With his other hand, he pulled Cynthia up to a sitting position. She was beginning to feel like a mindless puppet, numbed to everything save being pulled in this direction or that.

At Jonathan's encouragement, she opened the envelope and withdrew a letter, neatly handwritten on white stationery with the initials SMD imprinted on the front. Slowly, she read.

Dear Cynthia,

Please accept my most sincere congratulations on your engagement and pending marriage. Jonathan adores you and has for a long time now. I must admit that, distracted as he was in love, he was often trying to work with! But I think the world of him. He deserves the best . . . and I suspect he has it in you! Good luck and much happiness to both of you.

As Jonathan will have told you, our work together is just about done. As much as I am pleased with the outcome of Operation Lobster Trap, I am anxious to get back full time to Washington. My husband and twin sons have ordered that the next few weekends be reserved exclusively for them. As for me, I wouldn't have it any other way. I have missed them!

This charm was made by a goldsmith in Camden. I hope you will accept it as a token of my fondest regard and congratulations to two wonderful people. I believe you already have a chain!

Cynthia gazed in astonishment at the letter. Her husband . . . sons . . . most sincere congratulations . . . she felt a revival in her limbs and within an instant had propelled herself, finally and forever, into Jonathan's outstretched arms.

"I'm sorry . . . I'm sorry," she murmured against his chest, as the warmth from his body penetrated the cold shell she had built around her, shattering it to smithereeens.

He soothed her. "Shhh. You had no way of knowing," the velvet timbre of his deep voice fought her self-reproach.

She shook her head against him, even as his hand steadied it. "I should have known! You dropped so many hints. Why didn't I see? I'm so sorry, Jonathan!" She drew her head back to look longingly up at his strong features. When she spoke again, it was with the conviction of a newly gained insight.

"Jealousy is an ugly thing, isn't it?" Her brown lashes flickered almost imperceptibly as her gaze held his, so sure and steady.

Jonathan's response was a nonverbal one. Slowly, his lips descended until they met hers, firmly and sensuously conducting a masterful conversation of touching, tasting, giving, and receiving. Cynthia parted her lips to deepen the kiss, his muskiness and nearness reawakening her blunted senses.

"This has to stop," he growled huskily against her lips, reluctantly withdrawing from her, then smiling at her restored radiance. "That's better," he chuckled, gently kissing her forehead, as her brown orbs peered at him adoringly. She caught the twinkle in his eye as he suggested, "Why don't you open the box?"

It lay on the pine needles beside her. Shyly she lifted it and removed the pale blue ribbon and fresh white wrapping, aware of Jonathan's eyes following her every movement. She couldn't contain an exclamation of delight at the delicate gold lobster trap, no bigger than her thumbnail, which lay, finely etched and gleaming, on its cotton bed. At its center, enmeshed in strands of gold filigree, was a ruby, bright and red and sparkling.

"I—it's beautiful," she murmured softly, as she placed the exquisite charm in the palm of one ever-so-slightly trembling hand. "I don't deserve this," she whispered, lowering her head in shame.

Iron fingers were at her chin, raising her face until her gaze met and was held by those shimmering blue eyes. "Suzanne knew the pain you felt. She would have told you everything in a minute, if Cummings had only permitted it!" Jonathan's view touched on a lingering tear, which he promptly blotted with his thumb, tracing the line of her cheekbone as he did so.

Patiently, he explained further. "There were difficult times for Suzanne, too. She missed her family terribly while she was here, especially knowing that she was, for all practical purposes, incommunicado. Her great fear was that one of the twins would be hurt or get sick . . . they are only four years old!" He paused, his sandy hair falling casually over his forehead as he looked at the ground, reasoning aloud. "I think that it was our mutual torment that made us such good friends. When we weren't working, we spent the time consoling each other," he laughed, amused in hindsight at a situation that must have been anything but amusing at the time.

Cynthia was suddenly sidetracked as she realized that Jonathan had told her nothing of the operation itself. "I've read all the newspaper accounts, but tell me about your

183

part," she ordered, and he willingly complied, sharing events and details that the media, for one reason or another, had omitted, as well as embellishing on the ones that were already on public record.

"It looks like Dick will be the prosecution's star witness," he concluded, obviously pleased with that outcome.

"And what about you?" she cornered him. "Won't you have to testify?" The thought of losing him to this project for a moment longer infuriated her, but he quickly calmed her.

"Yes, but not extensively. Suzanne can handle most of it." Once again, Cynthia had Suzanne to thank. Guilt-ridden, she closed her fist on the charm. "I never really made much of an effort to get to know her . . ."

"You will," he smiled understandingly, his white teeth flashing in reflection of a ray of sun which had suddenly pierced the swaying branches above. At her look of puzzlement, he went on smugly. "I made Suzanne promise to spend a week or two up here next summer. Only, this time she'll take the lower cabin with her husband and the kids; we'll be in the upper one from now on! That is," he lowered his voice, and his eyes twinkled mischievously, "if you'll still have me . . ."

Cynthia raised her hands to caress his face, his hair, his neck, a look of wonderment becoming her features. "I'm the one who should be asking you that—"

"No more!" he interrupted, fondly gruff. "No more 'ifs,' no more excuses, no more apologies. Come here . . ." Bemused by his sudden authoritativeness, she leaned toward him, expecting another of his soul-searching kisses. She was taken by surprise when he lifted his hands to her neck and, in a heart-stopping moment for Cynthia, released the chain from her neck, deftly slipping the ring from it and into his hand.

Tenderly taking her left hand in his, he asked one last

184

time. "Will you be my wife, my dearest, dearest love?" A knot of happiness at her throat choked off all sound, precluding all but the nod of her head in silent acceptance of his proposal. Then, with a grace that sent an electrical current through her veins, he slipped the breathtaking diamond onto her ring finger, sealing their vows with it and with the impassioned kiss which followed.

But Jonathan had more on his mind than lovemaking. Prying her arms from their wrenchlike hold around his neck, he set her back onto the ground, simultaneously opening the fist that held the charm. Within an instant, he had threaded the gold chain through it and reclasped it around her neck, allowing the tiny lobster trap to bob against her chest. This act, too, he sealed with a kiss, one of exquisitely sweet torture, as he leaned forward and traced the circle of the necklace with his lips, deviating from the path here or there for a side nibble, leaving Cynthia in breathless frustration.

"Stop it . . . you're driving me crazy," she giggled in cover-up of her rising desires.

"An eye for an eye, so they say . . . it's only right that you should want me as I want you," he reasoned huskily, his tone reinforcing his words.

Brown lashes lowering bashfully over chocolate pools, she whispered, "You know I do! I've never before—"

Jonathan smoothly interrupted her confession, stroking her arms lovingly, "So I discovered during our moonlight swim. Did I ever tell you how beautiful you are?" He raised her face with his hands and kissed her features, one after the other, slowly and tenderly.

"And speaking of that night, I think it's about time I made an honest woman of you. As a matter of fact, I would have been back here earlier today, except for these arrangements. I had to pull a few strings, but here is our marriage license," he grinned in satisfaction at the look of excitement that lit her face at his words.

"When?" she asked breathlessly.

"How about tomorrow morning? At Dr. Moreland's house. It has all been arranged with the local justice. And," he added, his blue eyes taking on a special glitter, "I took the liberty of inviting your uncle—"

"Uncle William's coming?" she screamed excitedly, hugging him in response to the nod of affirmation that followed her question. "You've arranged everything!" she marveled, joy written all over her lightly tanned features.

Jonathan had yet more to tell. "Wait!" he raised a hand, as though to capture her attention, although knowing full well that it had been his throughout. "You haven't heard the rest. I've made reservations for a wedding luncheon at the yacht club in Camden, to be followed by a night here on Three Pines, while we close everything up." As Cynthia's gaze turned to one of perplexity, he completed the itinerary.

"The next morning we leave—at ten o' five, to be exact—from Augusta for New York, where we switch planes," he raised his eyebrows and turned his eyes upward in mocked attempt at recollection, "and board the four thirty flight for Paris. We'll spend some time in and around the French countryside before we return to New York after Labor Day." He paused, savoring Cynthia's astonished expression and suddenly speechless state. "Any comments, Professor?" he teased, a devilish cast to his features, streaked as they were by flickering rays of sun and shadow.

She returned his teasing. "I love it! But are you always going to take over and make all the arrangements without me?"

"Only when I get impulsive . . . the rest of the time you'll be an equal partner. But," he lowered his voice seductively, "you'll have to humor my whims once in a while . . . especially when it comes to indulging you!"

Cynthia nestled close to him, as he leaned back against

the broad and weathered trunk of the tallest of the three pines. A sinewy arm encompassed her shoulder, cementing their togetherness. She had, indeed, come home. This was where she belonged; this was where she wanted, more than any other place in the world, to be. In Jonathan's arms she could face the problems that life would inevitably send her way; in Jonathan's arms the many pleasures that life could hold would be immeasurably enhanced.

A sigh of contentment, soulful and sweet, escaped her lips. Yes, she thought, this had to be the most beautiful place in the world. With the vibrant reds and oranges of the sunset to the west, the invigorating midnight blue of the swelling ocean, and swaying to and fro as far as the eye could see to the east, the lush green needles and tangy pine essence of the stately giants towering above . . . and Jonathan, his heart beating steadily in her ear, its pulse hypnotic, his musky scent intoxicating, his rugged features magnetic, his very being reaching out to her with a promise of love, laughter, and fulfillment.

She was brought down to earth by a slight movement beside her as Jonathan shifted to gaze at her. "If you could only see your face, honey," he murmured, tracing the line of her cheek with his free hand. "That look of serenity . . . beatitude . . . it's as though you are off—," he waved his hand randomly upward into the air, "—in some heavenly paradise!" His smile was warm and he spoke an admiration which totally contradicted the arrogant mockery she would have expected several months ago. But now Cynthia traveled on his wavelength.

Her brown eyes smiled back at him with the intensity of understanding. "Oh, I *can* see my expression . . . it's mirrored here," and she lovingly feather-touched his features with her slender fingertips. "You must be on the same high," she marveled.

He held her gaze intently, the lights of utter adoration and unabashed desire mingling to spark anew his dazzling azure eyes. There was but the slightest hint of mischief in his velvet-smooth voice as he crooned intimately against her ear, "Now, if we hold onto one another very, very tightly," his arms closed around her in echo of his words, "we may keep this high forever . . ." His sensuous lips stilled, in tacit suggestion of sweetness to come.

Cynthia beamed beneath his tenderness, her heart brimming in utter ecstasy. "My thoughts exactly," she whispered, as she moved to join him in a mind-shattering, soul-reaching, love-proclaiming embrace.

Catch up with any Candlelights you're missing.

Here are the Ecstasies published this past November

ECSTASY SUPREMES $2.75 each

☐ 145 UNDERCOVER AFFAIR, Sydney Ann Clary.... 16426-5
☐ 146 THE WANDERER'S PROMISE, Paula Hamilton. 16918-6
☐ 147 LAYING DOWN THE LAW, Donna Kimel Vitek.. 19537-3
☐ 148 ROMAN FANTASY, Betty Henrichs............ 14605-4

ECSTASY ROMANCES $2.25 each

☐ 468 NO WAY TO TREAT A LADY, Jane Atkin...... 18823-7
☐ 469 PASSION AND POSSESSION, Kathy Clark.... 18310-3
☐ 470 WILD TEMPTATION, Helen Conrad.......... 19401-6
☐ 471 KING OF SEDUCTION, Alison Tyler.......... 19426-1
☐ 472 TRIPLE THREAT, Eleanor Woods............ 14653-4
☐ 473 SWEET TEMPEST, Ruth Smith............. 17451-1
☐ 17 WAGERED WEEKEND, Jayne Castle.......... 19413-X
☐ 21 LOVE'S ENCORE, Rachel Ryan.............. 14932-0

 At your local bookstore or use this handy coupon for ordering:

DELL READERS SERVICE—DEPT. B1335C
6 REGENT ST., LIVINGSTON, N.J. 07039

Please send me the above title(s) I am enclosing $ _____ (please add 75¢ per copy to cover postage and handling) Send check or money order—no cash or CODs Please allow 3-4 weeks for shipment

Ms./Mrs./Mr _____

Address _____

City/State _____ Zip _____